**Praise for
Carol Marinelli:**

'A heartwarming story about taking a chance and not
letting the past destroy the future. It is strengthened by
two engaging lead characters and a satisfying ending.'
—*RT Book Reviews* on
THE LAST KOLOVSKY PLAYBOY

'Carol Marinelli writes with sensitivity,
compassion and understanding, and
RESCUING PREGNANT CINDERELLA is not just a
powerful romance but an uplifting and inspirational tale
about starting over, new beginnings and moving on.'
—*Cataromance* on
ST PIRAN'S: RESCUING PREGNANT CINDERELLA

If you love Carol Marinelli,
you'll fall head over heels
for her sparkling, touching, witty debut
PUTTING ALICE BACK TOGETHER—
available from MIRA® Books

Step into the world of NYC Angels

Looking out over Central Park,
the Angel Mendez Children's Hospital,
affectionately known as Angel's,
is famed throughout America for being at the
forefront of paediatric medicine, with talented
staff who always go that extra mile for their
little patients. Their lives are full of highs,
lows, drama and emotion.

In the city that never sleeps, the life-saving
docs at Angel's Hospital work hard, play hard
and love even harder. There's *always* time for
some sizzling after-hours romance…

And striding the halls of the hospital,
leaving a sea of fluttering hearts behind him,
is the dangerously charismatic new head of
neurosurgery Alejandro Rodriguez. But there's
one woman, paediatrician Layla Woods, who's
left an indelible mark on his no-go-area heart.
Expect their reunion to be explosive!

NYC Angels

*Children's doctors who work hard and love
even harder…in the city that never sleeps!*

Dear Reader

New York City is my favourite place on earth. I love it, and one day want to spend a decent amount of time there. For that reason I was especially thrilled to be involved in this Medical Romance™ continuity set there.

I have loved working with wonderful authors and helping to create a series I really hope you enjoy.

Angel's Hospital is as busy as the city it is located in, and Jack and Nina kick the series off. I felt as if I knew Jack the second he came into my mind's eye, but Nina simply refused to conform to any preconceived image I had of her—which is rather how she is. Nina gave me a few surprises in the process of getting to know her.

She gave Jack a few, too.

Happy reading!

Carol Marinelli

NYC ANGELS: REDEEMING THE PLAYBOY

BY
CAROL MARINELLI

With love and thanks to Wendy S. Marcus x

First published in Great Britain 2013
by Mills & Boon, an imprint of Harlequin (UK) Limited.
Harlequin (UK) Limited, Eton House, 18-24 Paradise Road,
Richmond, Surrey TW9 1SR

© Harlequin Books S.A. 2013

Special thanks and acknowledgment are given to Carol Marinelli
for her contribution to the *NYC Angels* series

ISBN: 978 0 263 23351 3

CHAPTER ONE

'NINA WILSON.'

Jack kept his face impassive, but his cynical grey eyes rolled a little when he heard that Nina was the social worker who was dealing with baby Sienna's case.

Nina was hard work, and well Jack knew it, because they'd clashed on more than one occasion over the past couple of years.

Paediatrician Eleanor Aston had asked Jack, who was Head of Paediatrics, to join her in the case meeting that was to be held at nine this morning.

'The social work department seems intent on discharging Sienna home to the care of her parents,' Eleanor told him. 'I've been up nearly every night for a fortnight witnessing Sienna's withdrawal from methadone. The mother has already had two children taken off her. I personally looked after her newborn son last year.'

Eleanor's lips tightened at the memory of that time, but Jack chose not to notice. Instead, he flicked through the case notes as Eleanor's voice heightened with emotion, which Jack didn't respond to—he preferred facts. 'I just don't see why we're giving her a chance with her third baby when we know how she's been in the past.'

'You won't win with that argument against Nina

Wilson,' Jack said, and as he read through the notes he saw that some of them had, in fact, been written by him.

One entry that he had written was just over a week old: *Five-day-old, unsettled, distressed...* He'd been called by the night team for a consult, he noted, but as Jack tried to picture the baby he had written about just a few nights ago he felt a slight knot of unease that he couldn't place baby Sienna.

He told himself that it was to be expected—Angel Mendez Children's Hospital was a phenomenally busy free hospital in New York City. Not only did Jack head up the general paediatric team, he also dealt regularly with the board, Admin and the endless round of socialising and networking that was required to raise vital funds for the hospital.

The Carters were a prominent New York family and, as the son of a Park Avenue medical dynasty, Jack, with his endless connections and effortless grace, was called on often, not just for his impressive medical skills but also because of his connections and therefore the donations his family name alone could bring.

Still, this morning it was all about baby Sienna and making the best possible decisions for her future.

Jack finished with the medical history and read Nina's meticulous notes. They were very detailed and thorough and, Jack noted, very dispassionate—unlike Nina herself, who was incredibly fiery and fought hard for her patients. She was young, a little angry with bureaucracy and out to set the world to rights, whereas Jack, at thirty-four years of age, was just a touch more realistic as to what could and could not be achieved.

'Nina always comes down on the side of the parents,' Eleanor said.

'Not always.' Jack shook his head. 'Though I do know what you mean.'

He did.

Nina believed in families. Of course there were tough calls to be made at times and then she made them, but as Jack read through the notes he realised this was going to be a very long meeting.

Arguing with Nina was like an extremely prolonged game of tennis—everything that you served to her was returned with well-researched and thought-out force. He wasn't in the least surprised that Eleanor had asked him to sit in on the case meeting—Nina would know every inch of the family history and would have arguments and counter-arguments as to why her findings should be upheld.

'Come on, then.' Jack put on his jacket. He didn't need to check his appearance in the mirror—a combination of genes and wealth assured that he always looked good. His dark brown hair was trimmed fortnightly, his designer attire was taken care of by his housekeeper. All Jack had to do in the morning was kiss whatever lover was in his bed, head to the shower, shave and then step into his designer wardrobe to emerge immaculate a few moments later—more often than not just to break another heart.

As he headed to the meeting Jack thought briefly about Monica's tears that morning.

Why did women always demand a reason for why things had come to an end?

Why did they always want to know where they had

gone wrong or how they could change, or what had happened to suddenly change his mind?

Nothing had changed Jack's mind.

He simply didn't get involved and there was no such thing to Jack as long term.

And so, as he entered the meeting room, Jack readied himself for his second round of feminine emotion that morning. Nina had already arrived and was taking off her scarf and unbuttoning her coat. There were still a couple of flakes of snow in her hair and as she glanced over and saw him enter the room Jack watched her lips close tightly as she realised perhaps that Eleanor had brought in the big gun.

'Morning, Nina,' he greeted her, and flashed a smile just to annoy her.

'Jack.' Nina threw a saccharine smile in his direction and then turned her back and took off her coat.

Damn.

Nina didn't say it, of course, she just undid the belt and buttons and shrugged off her coat, but despite her together appearance she was incredibly unsettled and not just because Jack was Head of Paediatrics.

They clashed often.

Jack, always cool and detached, often brought her to the verge of tears, not that she ever let him see that. Just a couple of months ago she had been part of the team that had worked hard with a family struggling with a small baby who had been brought in to the emergency department. Jack had been reserved in his judgement that Baby Tanner should be discharged home to the care of the mother, but her team had fought hard to ensure that it happened. But just two weeks ago she had been called to the emergency department to find out that Baby Tanner had been brought in again, unconscious, a victim of shaken-baby syndrome.

Jack had said not one word to her as she had stepped into the cubicle.

His look had said everything, though—*I told you so*. Nina could still see his cool grey eyes harden as they had met hers, and she still carried the guilt.

But it wasn't just that that had Nina unsettled this morning.

Jack Carter was more than good looking and, of course, that didn't go unnoticed. He was known for his playboy ways and his charmed, privileged life, and the acquired arrogance that came with it irked Nina.

But, no, it wasn't just that either.

What really got to Nina was that *he* got to her.

He was arrogant, chauvinistic, dismissive—in fact, Jack Carter was everything Nina didn't like in a man, and, no, logically she didn't fancy him in the least—it was just that her body said otherwise.

It noticed him.

It reacted to him.

And Nina didn't like *it* one bit.

She could feel his eyes lazily watching her as she took off her coat, was incredibly aware of him as she hung up the garment and headed to the table to commence the meeting. She almost anticipated the slight inappropriateness that would undoubtedly come from his smirking lips.

He didn't disappoint her. 'Nice to see someone at the meeting with their clothes on,' Jack said as she made her way over, because everyone apart from Nina and

Jack was wearing scrubs. Everyone present laughed a little at his off-the-cuff remark.

Everyone, Jack noted, but Nina.

Then again, he'd never really seen her smile, at least not at him. She was always so serious, so intense and the only time her face relaxed and lit up with a smile was when she was engaging with her clients.

This morning she had on a grey pinafore dress with a red jumper beneath, but this was no school uniform! The red stockings and black boots that she wore took care of that. Nina's dark blonde hair was pinned up and her cheeks were red from coming into the warmth of the hospital from a very cold January morning.

'Sorry I'm late,' Nina said, taking a seat at the table opposite him. Just as Jack found himself wondering if the workaholic Nina had actually overslept, she corrected his thought process. 'I got called to go out on an urgent response.'

And, rather inconveniently for Jack, he wondered if there was a Mr Wilson who got annoyed at having Nina peeled from his bed at the crack of dawn by the emergency response team, or even a Ms Wilson, who bemoaned her partner leaving her side. Jack realised then that not once had Nina so much as flirted with him. Not once had she turned those cobalt-blue eyes to his in an attempt to bewitch him, which might sound arrogant, but flirting was par for the course when your name was Jack Carter.

Just never with Nina.

'Right.' Nina glanced around the table. Every person present felt like the enemy in this meeting and so she didn't bother to smile. 'Shall we get started, then?'

Nina really wasn't looking forward to this morning.

Normally she would have spent a lot of the weekend poring over the medical notes and histories, but she had been working at the pro bono centre as well as moving into her new three-bedroomed apartment. She'd hoped to get into work very early this morning and go over the notes again, but instead, at four a.m., just as her alarm clock had gone off, so too had her phone, and now Nina felt less than prepared.

Which was very unlike her.

Certainly, it didn't sit well with her. In a few short weeks her own family would be under the spotlight of a case conference and she wanted her sister and brother's case worker to be as passionate and as informed as she usually was. Still, even if Nina hadn't prepared as meticulously as usual, she was still well informed and, given Sienna was only two weeks old, most of the details of the case were fresh in her mind.

She knew that most of the medical staff were opposed to Sienna being discharged home to the parents. Their concerns had been well voiced and they were repeated again now.

First she heard from Brad Davis, head of the prenatal unit. Brad had seen Hannah for her very brief prenatal care and had also delivered Sienna, but thankfully he was very matter-of-fact in his summing up.

'Hannah presented to us at thirty-four weeks gestation,' Brad explained. 'She had recently resumed her relationship with Sienna's father, Andy. He was seemingly the one who insisted that Hannah attend Angel's. Andy was concerned about Hannah's drug habit and the effect it would have on their unborn child—Hannah's only concern was feeding her habit.'

'At that time,' Nina responded, and Brad nodded. 'She complied with the methadone programme?' Nina asked, and again Brad nodded, and so on they went.

Nina heard from the midwives and nursing staff and also the addiction counsellors who had been in regular contact with Hannah.

Eleanor Aston, though, was particularly difficult. Always a huge advocate for her patients, Eleanor was perhaps the most insistent that Sienna be removed from her mother's care.

'I looked after her son last year.' Eleanor's voice shook with emotion. 'And I can remember—'

'We're not discussing Sienna's half-brother this morning,' Nina interrupted. She knew that it was terribly difficult to separate the two cases, especially as Eleanor had dealt with Hannah at her very worst and had looked after what had indeed been a very sick little baby boy with a very cold and unfeeling mother, but this was a crucial part of Nina's job and one that made her less than popular at times with the medical staff.

'The difference this time around is that Hannah is doing her best to get straight and she is also in a very different relationship with this baby's father. As soon as Andy found out that Hannah was pregnant he brought her straight to Angel's and has been rigorously making sure that she keeps up with the programme, and Hannah herself has made a huge effort—'

'When?' They were half an hour into the meeting and it was the first time that Jack had actually spoken. He looked across the table at Nina as he did so.

'When exactly did Hannah make this huge effort that you keep talking about?'

'Since she came to Angel's.' Nina's voice was very calm. She had been expecting Jack to step in at any moment and she hadn't been proved wrong.

'She had nine months to dry out,' Jack said, and then corrected himself. Nina was quite sure Jack's mistake was deliberate. 'Oh, sorry, make that eight months, because it was considered vital that we induce her early due to the baby's failure to thrive in the womb.' Still he stared at Nina, perhaps waiting for her to interrupt, or to speak over him, but she met his cool gaze without words of her own and Jack carried on.

'So, all in all, she actually managed two weeks of antenatal care, mainly because of her boyfriend's efforts, and then two weeks of *huge* effort postnatally, but only with every system and resource available in place.'

'Your point being?' Nina asked, and Jack didn't answer. 'Why wouldn't we offer every resource that we have to this family?' She watched his jaw tighten as she scored a point.

'Hannah has been attending addiction counselling twice daily. For the first time she actually wants all the help and support that we can provide and there is also an extremely devoted father who, I am quite sure, will put the baby's welfare first. Hannah has broken down with me on two separate occasions and told me that she doesn't want another child taken off her and that she is prepared to do whatever it takes. Now, I know that this is early days—'

'My doctors have been up with that baby night after night,' Jack interrupted. 'I personally have been called

in when Sienna has become agitated and distressed.'
His eyes held Nina's and she didn't blush or blink but
simply met his gaze. 'The baby had severe withdrawal,
she was small for her dates due to maternal malnour-
ishment, just like her older brother, and it is my opinion that the last person the baby—'

'Sienna,' Nina interrupted. 'The baby is called Sienna and to date there is nothing that I have seen,
from my many observations, to indicate that any of
the traits that were a cause for concern with her other
children are present now, and the nursing observations
verify that....'

Jack drew a long breath as Nina spoke on. Her holistic approach irked him, and he sat, turning his heavy
pen over and over as he listened to Nina drone on about
how damaging it would be to both Sienna and Hannah if they were separated now, especially as a strong
bond had been established. Jack said nothing, though
he wanted to point out that a bond surely took longer
than a couple of weeks, but he knew he'd be shot down,
not just by Nina but by everyone in the room.

Jack really didn't get the maternal bond argument.

His pen turned in his fingers as he thought for a moment of his own mother—she certainly hadn't had one.
Instead, Jack had been assigned to two nannies and had
only been brought down for dinner and social events.

But instead of dwelling on his own messed-up family, he listened how, from Nina's findings, there was
nothing to indicate at this stage that Sienna was at risk
and that with full back-up and aftercare, the department
had determined that the child should be discharged to
the care of the parents.

'So what am I here for, then?' Jack challenged. 'From a medical point of view the baby has put on sufficient weight to be discharged, she is stable, her withdrawal from methadone is manageable now and you've clearly already determined the outcome. You're really not interested in hearing our concerns—'

'Don't!' For the first time this meeting Jack heard the shake of anger in Nina's voice. 'Don't you dare insinuate that I am dismissing the medical staff's concerns.'

Jack rolled his tongue in his cheek. He certainly wasn't about to apologise, but inwardly he conceded that perhaps he had gone a bit too far. At the end of the day the social services department did one hell of a job. They dealt with the most vulnerable children and handled the most difficult cases and had to make decisions that few would relish, so he sat silent as Nina spoke on.

'Every one of your concerns has been listened to and addressed. Every point you have made has been noted.' Nina looked around the table. 'I have to take each case on its own merits and in *this* case I see the mother making a huge effort. She is racked with guilt, witnessing all that Sienna is going through, and—' Nina looked over at Eleanor '—while I accept that she had none of those feelings with the other two children, in this instance it is very different.

'There is a father who is stepping up and a couple who are desperate to keep their child but, yes, there is also a baby who, thanks to her mother's poor choices, has had an appalling start to life. Now, I could arrange temporary placement for Sienna, but I can assure you the foster-care system is not a fairy-tale alternative, especially when we believe that, with support, this family does have a chance.'

'Well,' came Jack's terse response, 'I've voiced my concerns.'

'They've been noted.'

As soon as the meeting concluded Jack stood. 'If you'll excuse me.'

Once outside Eleanor spoke with him briefly. 'Thanks so much for trying, Jack.'

'Nina made several good points.' Jack said to Eleanor, because although he always went in to bat for his staff he could play the devil's advocate better than anyone, but probably, in this instance, he actually agreed with Nina. 'I know that it's hard to step back at times...'

'It doesn't seem that way for you.' Eleanor sighed.

'Yeah, well, you have to be tough to do this job or you'd go crazy,' Jack said. 'Eleanor, sometimes you just have to look at the facts. In this case the mother is doing everything right, albeit too little too late, but, as Nina said, if we take this child from the mother now then realistically they are not going to reunite and though we might think that that might be for the best, who knows where Sienna might end up?'

'She might be placed with the perfect family. She might...' Eleanor started, but her lips tightened and her words halted as Nina came out.

'There's no such thing as the perfect family,' Jack said, and giving Nina a brief nod he stalked off.

'Says the man who comes from one.' Eleanor rolled her eyes as Jack walked off and then stood a little awkwardly when it was clear that Nina was hanging around to speak to her. 'Did you see the Carter family Christmas photo shoot?'

Nina gave a pale smile. Yes, she'd seen it—all the Carters gathered around the hospital Christmas tree, their diamonds gleaming as much as their capped smiles. There had recently been a magazine spread too on Jack's parents, but she didn't want to think about Jack now so Nina got straight to the difficult point. 'I'm sorry that you're upset about the department's decision.'

'Thanks.' Nina watched as Eleanor's eyes filled up behind her glasses as she spoke. 'I've listened to all that you've said and I've just spoken with Jack and he's right—you made some very good points. It's just that I saw what Hannah was like with her son. She was so distant and unfeeling and refused to take any responsibility...'

'Addiction will do that every time,' Nina said.

'I know.' Eleanor nodded.

'And I can assure you that we will be watching Sienna very carefully. The real difference in this case is that there is a loving father on the scene. I really feel that if Hannah goes back to her ways of old and starts using again, then Andy will be the one raising Sienna...'

'Far from perfect.'

'Not so far from perfect.' Nina smiled. 'I think that he'd do a great job.'

As she said goodbye to Eleanor and headed off to find Hannah to let her know about the meeting, she paused for a moment by the water cooler and took a drink, Eleanor's words still replaying in her mind.

Jack Carter thought she had made several good points.

Because she *had* made several good points, Nina told herself, screwing up the small plastic cup and tossing it into the waste bin.

She didn't need his admiration, neither did she need his approval.

The only opinion Nina wanted from Jack was a professional one.

She just had to remember that fact.

CHAPTER TWO

WITH THE MEETING over Jack walked through the maternity unit, restless, angry but not sure why. He was looking forward to getting back to the shield of his office, but his pager stopped him and he halted to use the phone. However, as he waited to be connected by the switchboard he glanced at the handover sheet one of the nurses was working on.

Sienna Andrews. He saw the room she was in and the doctor she was under, that she had been the third pregnancy, and in the comments section was written 'NASS'—which stood for neonatal abstinence scoring system, a method used to gauge a newborn's withdrawal from the drugs they had been subjected to in what should have been the safety of the womb.

Jack concluded his call and walked through the maternity ward, pausing when he came to the room where Sienna was. He looked through the glass to the row of isolettes. Hannah wasn't with her daughter, though a nurse was there, tending to the baby. Jack rarely went into these rooms, only when it was necessary.

Angel's was a free hospital—there was more hope and heartbreak than one building could contain and as Head of Paediatrics Jack had more than enough to contend with, without getting unnecessarily involved with each and every case.

He had to stay detached, which he did easily.

Jack had learnt the art of detachment long before he had studied medicine—he'd been told by his parents to toughen up at a very young age, and told it over and over again, and so he had, simply refusing to hand over his emotions to anyone.

He had this sudden strange vision of Nina chairing a meeting about his own family and it brought a wry smile to his lips.

There *was* no such thing as a perfect family.

Certainly he never discussed his family life with any of his many lovers—he didn't let anyone close and maintained the Carter image, because the image could be used for good. Jack looked around the unit, saw the cots and the equipment and, ever practical, thought of the cost.

'Do you need anything, Jack?' Cindy, one of the nurses, broke into his thoughts.

'Nope.' Jack shook his head. 'I'm just checking in. How's baby Andrews doing?'

'She's doing really well,' Cindy said, as Jack looked through Sienna's charts. 'She's still a little irritable at times, but seems much more settled now. She'd put on another ounce when we weighed her this morning and mum's given her a bath. How did the case conference go?'

'Same old, same old.' Jack shrugged. 'Home to the parents, follow-up, support systems in place...' He looked at Cindy, who had worked at Angel's for a very long time. They'd slept together once, years ago, but there was no awkwardness between them. Cindy was now happily married and expecting her first baby and Jack valued her opinion a lot. 'What do you think?'

'As I said in my notes, mum's really making an effort…'

'But what do *you* think?'

'That I hope her effort lasts.'

Cindy walked off to check on a baby that was crying and Jack looked down into the cot, stared into the babe's dark blue eyes and wondered, not for the first time lately, if he was in the right job.

Of course the hospital wanted him, he worked sixty-hour weeks as well as juggling a social life that would have most people exhausted. He did an excellent job with the staff, as well as the extracurricular events that ensured the city's goodwill for the hospital continued.

He did a great job.

He just didn't love it.

Didn't know how to fire up, the way Nina had.

He'd heard the tremble in her voice, the passion she had for the family, her willingness to go against the flow and fight for a cause. Sometimes, and this was one of those times, he wished he had even a tenth of her passion.

He looked at Sienna, hoped that for her Angel's had done its best. She'd had the best doctors, nurses, social workers, but would it be enough?

He turned as Nina came into the room.

'How is she?' Nina asked, wondering if he had been called for a problem.

'Fine.'

'Is Hannah around?' Nina asked.

'Nope, I think she's at one of her meetings...'

'That's fine,' Nina said. 'I just wanted to go through the meeting and the conclusions with her.' She walked over to the cot and gave a slightly wary smile to Jack. She wasn't particularly used to seeing him pensive by a cot. 'I was just explaining to Eleanor that we'll be arranging regular—'

'I'll read about it, thanks.'

'Of course you will.'

Nina saw his jaw tighten at her response and she smothered a smile that twitched on her lips as she scored an unfair point. But that was what Jack did— oh, she had no doubt at all that he was a brilliant doctor, he was incredibly respected amongst his peers and she knew that he was considered a brilliant diagnostician.

She'd seen him in action on several occasions, all suited and suave, and then, when he'd delivered his opinion, when the crisis was over, when he'd saved another life, the next time Nina might see him was the way she had this morning in a meeting.

'All the resources that you're putting in place for Sienna and her family...' Jack's voice was steel. 'Where do you think they come from?'

Nina gave a tight shrug. She probably had gone a bit far—she had just wanted to needle him a bit, pay him back for his words in the meeting, and now, clearly, she had.

Jack gave Nina a brief nod and headed off, taking the lift down and walking towards Emergency, where he was meeting with one of hospitals most prominent benefactors.

He was sick of it.

Sick of the smooth talk, sick of the smarming just to get a decent-sized cheque.

Maybe it *was* time for a change.

Thanks to his extremely privileged upbringing and some very astute investments, Jack could easily not work another day in his life.

But then what?

Maybe he should follow in his father's footsteps. Set up his own private Park Avenue practice, screen and choose his patients, patch them up and send them on their way.

A practice where he could fix everything.

Get in at nine.

Do a good job.

Be thanked.

Go home at six.

To what?

'Incoming storm.' As he walked along the corridor Jack was jolted out of his dark thoughts by the sound of a familiar voice.

'Alex!' He shook his colleague's hand. 'It's good to see you—first day?'

'It is.' Alex nodded.

'And?'

'It's going well,' Alex said.

They had trained together at medical school, where two very ambitious minds had met and had got on well from the start, both admiring the determination in the other—two men who had not settled for a pass mark, two men who had been determined to excel. Jack had chosen the speedier route of paediatrics, while Alex

Rodriguez had chosen neurosurgery and had just been appointed head of that department at Angel's.

Jack had used his weight there too in employing his friend—Alex's skills hadn't been the issue, though, more a dark shadow on Alex's past that the board had deliberated over. 'I actually wanted to come and speak to you to say thank you for the recommendation.'

'You didn't need my recommendation,' Jack said. 'You were very impressive at the interviews—Angel's wants you on board.'

'Thanks.' Alex was quiet for a moment. 'And I am grateful to the board for agreeing not to bring up...' His voice trailed off—Alex didn't need to go into detail with Jack, there had been a messy court case in Los Angeles a few years ago that the board had finally agreed to keep confidential. Jack knew it had nearly destroyed Alex, and not just professionally. Still, Jack also knew that there was no one better for the role.

'The past is the past.'

'Yep.' Alex wasn't exactly known for small talk, but just as they were about to head off, Alex spoke on. 'Everything okay with you, Jack?'

'Me?'

'Incoming storm.' Alex's smile was wry. 'I could see it approaching as you walked towards me—it's not the Jack I know.'

'Yeah, well, you've been in Australia for five years. Maybe the Jack you used to know is getting older...' He ran a hand through his hair. 'I've just sat through a case meeting with the most annoying social worker...' Jack rolled his eyes. 'You know the type.'

'Holistic approach?' Alex said, and Jack gave a reluctant smile. 'With the right services in place...' Alex put on his best social worker voice and Jack actually laughed. 'They're the same the world over. Still, can you imagine this job without them?'

'No,' Jack admitted. 'Anyway, right now I've got to go and do some sweet-talking—there's a VIP waiting for a private tour of Emergency.' Jack's words dripped sarcasm. 'I can't wait.'

Maybe it wasn't Social Services that was getting to him, maybe it was this place, or maybe, Jack thought as he saw a pair of red-stockinged, black-booted legs walking very briskly along the corridor, her pager trilling, with Security by her side, it was one social worker in particular.

'Problem?' Jack checked as she dashed past him, but she just gave him a very strange look at his question. Nina didn't generally get fast-paged because things were going well in the world.

And she had *really* hoped for Tommy and his father, Mike, that things were finally starting to go well.

'Just stay back,' Nina said to the security guards as they took the lift to the psychology wing. 'Mike gets very angry at times, but it's all hot air. I'll tell you if I need you to intervene.'

She was met by Linda, one of the most senior child psychologists. 'I've got another worker in with them at the moment,' Linda said, and then explained what had happened that morning. 'Basically, I noticed Tommy had a nasty cut on his hand. It was covered by a bandage but it came off during play therapy and it looks infected. I think it should have had stitches, but when I suggested we bring Tommy down to Emergency to have it looked at, Mike refused. He got extremely angry and now he's insisting on taking Tommy straight home.'

'How's Tommy?'

'Pale...' Linda said. 'Listless. He's lost weight too. I saw him just last month and everything seemed fine. Things have been going so well between them...'

'I was hoping to close the case this week,' Nina admitted. 'Obviously with ongoing support for Tommy...' She bit back on the expletive that was rising in her throat. She had been sure that things were so much better, had been sure there wasn't a protective issue, and then she heard Mike shouting.

'We're going home.' He had Tommy in his arms and was striding down the corridor. 'Oh, not you!' he shouted when he saw Nina. 'Got your bodyguards with you?'

'Mike.' Nina was calm but firm. 'Tommy needs to have that cut seen. If it's infected, he will need—'

'I'll stop at the drug store on the way home.' Mike didn't let her finish, just marched on towards the lifts.

'Mike...' She walked alongside him, and as he jumped into a lift that was going up, Nina darted in and the doors closed before Security could get in too.

Mike continued his angry rant, not caring that there was a family with a child in a wheelchair, not noticing Alex Rodriguez, who was in the lift and about to intervene. Nina glanced at his ID and realising he worked at Angel's gave a brief shake of her head. In a confined space it might only make things worse.

'We can talk properly down in Emergency,' Nina said to Mike, because the last thing she wanted was Mike walking off in this mood with his son.

'I'm sick of your talking!' Mike shouted.

'You're scaring Tommy.' She watched as Mike screwed up his face, watched as he tried to contain himself for his son, and thankfully Alex made sure everyone but himself got out at the next floor.

She was grateful to Alex for sticking around while staying back as they walked briskly to Emergency, Security catching up just as they got to the entrance doors.

It was a busy Monday morning in Emergency, Jack noted. He actually wanted to take off his suit jacket and pitch in, but instead he was stuck showing Elspeth Hillier around and telling her what her huge donation, in memory of her late husband, was earmarked for.

'We're hoping to have a supervised play area…' Jack explained. 'It would be used for the siblings of the patient or any child in the care of their guardian. Often the parent or carer arrives with two or three children in tow—naturally they want to be with their child throughout procedures and interviews, instead of having to take care of the other children until help arrives. The patient misses out on the comfort of the carer or, more often than not, the nurses end up babysitting.'

'And it would be called…' Elspeth asked.

'We haven't decided on a name yet,' Jack said. 'But certainly it would be something that honours the Hillier name.'

'Not for me, of course,' Elspeth said. 'I just want Edgar to be remembered.'

'Of course,' Jack duly replied, though he was quite sure it wouldn't be called the Edgar child-care centre or the Edgar Hillier child-care centre... He knew the routine only too well; he'd been raised on it after all.

'So when will building commence?' Elspeth asked, but Jack didn't answer. He was distracted for a moment, not because of a new outbreak of commotion—that was commonplace here—but more at the sight of those red stockings again. Nina was walking through the department alongside a gentleman who was holding a pale-looking child. They were flanked by two security guards and Alex Rodriguez was present too.

Jack tried to answer Elspeth's question but his eyes kept wandering to the group and he watched as a nurse approached to take the child.

'Excuse me for a moment, Elspeth...'

Security were bracing themselves, Alex was hovering, nurses were looking over, and any second now the button would be pressed for the police to be called as the father was becoming more and more agitated. Only Nina stood resolute and calm. He could see her speaking to the gentleman and, as Jack approached, he saw that whatever she had said had worked, for without further demur he handed the child over to a nurse.

Jack was about to head back to Elspeth and even Alex had turned to go when the explosion hit. 'Who the hell do you think you are, bitch?' The man was right in Nina's face, cursing her and, despite the presence of Security, backing Nina into a cubicle. But even then her voice was, to Jack's ears, annoyingly calm, telling the security officers to step back.

'I can handle this, thank you.'

Er, actually, no, she couldn't, Jack was quite sure. There was well over six feet of angry male yelling at her, telling her that he had trusted her, that she should know him better, that he would never harm his child.

'Take a seat, Mike.' She just stood in the middle of the cubicle as he ranted. 'No one is accusing you of anything, but Tommy looks unwell and needs to be examined. He has a cut that appears infected. No one has said anything about you harming your son.'

'You're nothing but a—'

'Enough.' Jack stepped in between them. 'I'm Jack Carter, Head of Paediatrics. Can I ask what is going on?'

'I've got this, thanks, Jack.' He heard her bristling with anger and held back the slight incredulous shake of his head, because her anger was aimed at him! Still, he happily ignored Nina and looked at the man.

'Sir?' Jack stood patiently, his eyes warning the other man to calm down, and slowly he seemed to a little, but his words were still angry when he answered.

'Tommy had an appointment today with the child psychologist and everything seemed fine but then they decide that the cut on his hand needs to be seen. I just want to take him home, he's tired, and then *she* arrives with security guards in tow and I'm hauled down here just because a four-year-old has a cut hand.'

'It looks infected,' Nina stated. 'It needs to be checked, it's that simple, Mike.'

'How did he get the cut?' Jack asked.

'I don't know.' Mike's temper reared again. 'He's four years old, they fall over all the time.'

'Sure they do.' Jack nodded. 'I'll go and take a look at him myself right now. The thing I want you to do is to calm down before you go in to see him. You've scared your son—he doesn't need to see his father angry and upset.' He gave a brief nod to Nina, who stepped outside with him.

'It's a very complicated history—' she started.

'I'm sure that it is,' Jack interrupted, 'but right now my concern is the child's medical status.'

'The father can be explosive at times, but he's never been that way with his child...'

Jack didn't want to hear her findings at this stage. His only thought was for the safety of the child—well, there was one other thing he would address later. 'I'm going to speak to you afterwards about your own safety. I don't want staff taking risks.'

'I know the family. I knew what I was doing—'

'I'm not arguing about this right now,' Jack broke in. 'I'll speak to you later.'

'If I can just explain about Tommy...'

'Please, don't. Right now I want to go and see that child and find out first hand what we're dealing with.'

So quickly Jack dismissed her.

Other times he blamed her.

But right now she couldn't think about Dr Perfect Never Make A Mistake Carter. Instead she turned to another man, one who had made an awful lot of mistakes that morning, and she watched as Mike sat down, put his head in his hands and started to sob.

'I didn't mean to scare him.' He was beside himself. 'Tommy will be petrified without me...'

'I know that,' Nina said. 'What's going on, Mike?'

'Nothing.'

'When did Tommy get the cut?'

'I don't know, a few days ago... I need to be with him.'

'Not yet. I want you to sit here for a while. Someone will bring you a drink and when things are more settled I'll come and speak to you.'

'I should be with him.'

'You can't be with him because you just lost your temper, Mike!' Despite what Jack might think, Nina was no pushover. 'You can't be with your son because you refused to bring him down for an examination, because you avoided Security and then bullied me into a cubicle. You blew this, Mike, so, no, right now you can't be with him. I'll go in. Tommy knows me, I'll stay with him for now...'

Nina left the cubicle and asked a nurse where Tommy was and was pointed in the direction. She knocked on the examination-room door and was let in.

'Good timing.' She could hear the weary bitterness in his voice. 'I was just about to call you with an urgent referral.' She looked down at Tommy, who was being helped into a gown that was covered with cartoon characters. Nina looked at his pale, bruised body and immediately she could see why she was about to be called. Then she looked over at Jack and she saw it again.

The look he had given her when she had walked into Baby Tanner's cubicle.

The look he would give her if Sienna returned unwell to the department.

It was a look she knew all to well, and one Jack Carter gave her all too often.

I told you so.

CHAPTER THREE

'EXCUSE ME A minute, Tommy.' Jack stepped outside and Nina assumed that she was meant to follow, but of course she had it wrong. Instead, Jack spoke with an elderly, very elegant woman, who looked less than impressed when he headed back towards Tommy's cubicle, offering Nina a brief explanation. 'Lewis is stuck with a multi-trauma, I'm just waiting for the registrar to come and take over. I just want to make sure that there's nothing medically urgent that is wrong.'

'Can I just have a brief word before you go in, Jack?' He gave a slight hiss of frustration as he turned around. 'Tommy is a very guarded child. Initially he had nothing to do with his father and responded only to me, but over the past months…'

She didn't finish; instead she watched as Jack's grey eyes shuttered as they so often did when she spoke. 'You don't want to hear what I have to say?'

'At this stage, no. I want to find out from the child what has happened and given that you have had dealings with the family and that Tommy seems to trust you, I'd like you to assist. Do you think you can?'

'Of course, but—'

'I like facts Nina,' he interrupted. 'I like to explore

things for myself and I do not want to walk in there with my thought process crowded by yours.'

'Sure.'

He was arrogant, dismissive, even rude, but there was no mistaking that he was brilliant with Tommy. He didn't rush in, he just chatted to the little boy for a couple of minutes and then asked him something about his parents.

'Tommy's mum is deceased,' Nina said quietly, and had he given her just one moment to speak he might not be feeling such an insensitive bastard right now. At least, Nina hoped that was what he was thinking.

Of course it wasn't.

Jack had been rather hoping Tommy might speak a little for himself, but instead he sat silent and pale, his mop of dark curls unkempt and unwashed. He had dark circles under his eyes and, Jack noted, despite gentle prompting, he remained silent.

'Okay, Tommy,' Jack said, pulling on his gloves, 'we're just going to take a look at that cut of yours.' He looked at Nina and for the first time that day he was smiling in her direction—for the sake of the patient, of course. 'You know Nina, I hear.'

Tommy's eyes darted towards her and she gave him a smile. 'We've met a few times, haven't we, Tommy?' Nina walked over and looked at the cut. It was deep and infected and it was clear that it should have been medically dealt with at the time it had happened. 'That looks sore,' Nina said. 'What happened?' She saw the confusion in Tommy's eyes. 'It's okay,' Nina said. 'We just want to find out what happened so we can make sure it gets better.'

'Where's Dad?' The question was aimed at Nina, and it was the first words Jack had heard Tommy say.

'Dad's just having a seat and a drink in another area.' She made it clear, Jack noted, that his dad was well away and that he could talk freely, and she asked him again about the cut.

'I don't know.'

Gently Jack examined him, probing his little stomach, exploring his rib cage, noting that Tommy winced when he did so. Jack pulled on his stethoscope and listened to Tommy's chest, but looked up as someone stepped into the cubicle.

'Sorry about that.' A woman smiled. 'I'm Lorna Harris, locum registrar.'

'It's fine Lorna, I've got this,' Jack dismissed, but then a nurse popped her head around the door and explained that Elspeth was getting impatient.

Jack closed his eyes in mounting frustration. He opened them to two very dark blue ones and the serious face of Nina, and for the first time that morning he said what was on his mind. 'Do you know what I hate about charity?'

His voice was low and for Nina's ears only, the words not even for her really, they just came from a dark place inside him called frustration, not that she could understand. Jack never expected her to answer. He was already pulling off his gloves, and he certainly never thought that she might get it, but at the sound of her voice he stilled.

'The cost?'

Jack gave a wry smile, noted the small circles of colour rise on her cheeks as still he kept looking. He would have loved to continue this conversation, would have loved to say more, but the world outside waited. He turned and apologised to Tommy, told the little guy that Lorna would take good care of him now.

'Will I see you again later?' Tommy suddenly asked.

Jack had many noncommittal answers that he used to reply to questions such as this one, but apart from Nina he was the only person Tommy had spoken to, and though Jack did his best not to get too pulled in, especially with cases as emotional as this one, for reasons he didn't want to explore, yes, he would be following up on this case.

In detail.

'I'll come and check on you later, but it probably won't be till tonight,' Jack said. 'So you may already be asleep.'

Certainly Tommy was going to be admitted.

He handed over his findings to Lorna and then stepped out. Nina found herself blushing and unsettled by their brief conversation and just the effect of Jack Carter close up. He unsettled her in many areas— filthy rich, filthy morals, combined with a brilliance that somehow, despite his title, was wasted.

She'd always thought him shallow; a spoiled rich boy playing doctor, but she had sensed that he really wanted to be in here with Tommy, not out there talking with a benefactor, and for the first time she wondered if it was always so easy for him. Not that she had long to dwell on it. Despite gentle questioning, Tommy could offer no explanation for the cut and the bruising.

'Yes.' He started to cry when he admitted that his

dad had been really cross that morning when he had wet the bed again.

Tommy had stopped wetting the bed three months ago.

Lorna was nice to Tommy, but not as thorough as Nina found Jack to be, and despite Nina telling her the complicated history, it was clear by the time they went into speak with Mike, Lorna had already made her mind up.

'As tragic as their history is,' Lorna said after interviewing Mike, 'we have a child with injuries neither he nor the father can account for, a nasty, infected cut that the father has not sought help for and a father that is hostile and angry towards staff. He already has a history with Child Protection.'

'I've explained why.'

'I know you have, but he's also admitted how frustrated he is that Tommy has started wetting the bed again.' She paused as they were told Tommy's X-rays were in, and as she checked them Nina's heart sank. 'Two fractured ribs.'

They spoke at length and a child abuse screen was ordered—bloods would be taken and a full skeletal survey done, and in the meantime Nina would obtain an order that the father could only visit Tommy while supervised.

It was a long, busy day—the emergency with Tommy was just added to her routine work and by the time Nina had caught up with Sienna the clock was nudging nine p.m., but still there was work to do.

Nina had had a long conversation with Mike, and, despite all evidence pointing to him, something simply didn't sit right with her. Tommy had been desperately upset when his father had left, and Nina had assured Mike that there would be a case worker available first thing in the morning to supervise his access. Then she headed back into the general ward, where Tommy had been admitted, and went over and spoke to him, reassuring him that he was okay and that his father would be back in the morning.

Jack was sitting in the small office, going through Tommy's notes, and he looked up as Nina entered the darkened ward. Her hair, which had been rather more neatly pinned up that morning, had bit by bit worked its way out of the pins and fallen in soft tendrils around her face. She must be exhausted, Jack thought, remembering that she had been called out for an emergency even before that morning's meeting.

He wondered again if there was a Mr Wilson, though, remembering the blush that had spread on her cheeks that moment when their eyes had locked, he was certain that there was no Ms Wilson.

He was so not going there! Jack looked down at the notes he was reading—the last thing he needed was a fling with someone as intense as Nina Wilson.

Don't even think about it. Jack grinned to himself.

Maybe his own lack of sleep was catching up with him.

Still, he did find himself looking at her again, saw that she was in no rush with Tommy, and wondered how she had the mental energy to be so involved.

And then she looked over towards the office and caught his eye, and Jack, for once, felt a little uncomfortable, as if he'd been caught staring. But he didn't look away, just watched as she made her way over to him.

'Nina.' He gave her a nod and he noted that she closed the door behind her.

'Could I have a word with you?'

'Sure.'

'I'm worried.' She gave him a tight smile. 'Which is nothing new. I always am...but tonight I'm really worried.'

'Go on.'

'I've just spent another couple of hours talking to Mike and I've just been in again to Tommy and I just don't think that Mike's responsible for the bruising.' She looked at him. 'Have you read the notes?'

'I've just started.'

'Have you read my notes?'

'Not yet.' Part of Jack's frustration was that he never actually got a chance to sit down and do that. He was always relying on handovers, catching up. He had read Lorna's findings and wasn't quite happy with the detail of her notes, would have preferred to have thoroughly examined Tommy himself rather than rely on a locum registrar's findings. He looked at Nina, saw the tension in her face and her genuine concern. 'Tell me what you know.'

She actually exhaled in relief before she started talking. 'I've been working with the family for six months, since the mother's death,' Nina explained. 'Prior to Kathy's death, the marriage was in trouble—they had major financial issues and Mike was away all week working, and when he came home at weekends Kathy often went to her mother's, so he hardly saw Tommy.

Six months ago, Mike left for a trip after a huge argument with Kathy. He didn't ring her that day, but the next day, when he did, she didn't answer her phone and he figured she still wasn't talking to him.

'When she still didn't pick up the next day, Mike had a neighbour go and check on her. She was dead and Tommy was with her, hungry and dehydrated...'

Jack wasn't shocked, he had heard many stories like this before, but he saw tears well up in her eyes and her involvement in the case unnerved him, challenged him even. 'Given the row and the circumstances, there was suspicion as to Mike's involvement in the death. While Tommy was admitted here, the father was flying back to face police questioning, and Child Protection was naturally called in. That's the reason for my involvement.'

'Okay.' His expression was deadpan, but his mind filtered the information, and, Nina noted, he really was listening.

'Tommy had shut down from the trauma of being with his mother's body, but apart from that there were issues with bonding with his father.'

'Explain.'

She smiled. He didn't waste words, but gave her a chance to speak.

'When I first met Tommy and his father, Tommy took all his direction from me. He had more connection with me than with his own father. As you know, a child is normally unsure around strangers, but not in this case. Mike had had very few dealings with Tommy and that's what we've been working on, whereas the psychologist has been dealing more with the issues of losing his mother. They've come on in leaps and bounds—despite enormous financial stress, Tommy and Mike are a real unit. He looks to his father now for prompts, he's asking to see him right now...'

'The father clearly has a temper problem. I saw the way he was with you.'

'Yes,' Nina said. 'But never with Tommy.'

'Never?'

'He was cross this morning about the wet bed, but that was out of frustration and fear. He doesn't understand the bruises and the cut. Mike told me that he was terrified that we'd take him away, what we'd think, that's why he didn't bring him in—which, yes, was a terrible call...'

Jack nodded. It had been a terrible call but one he had seen many parents make.

'I remember one child that was referred to us for unexplained bruising had leukaemia...'

'He's had blood work.' Jack shook his head. 'He hasn't got that and leukaemia wouldn't account for two fractured ribs and an infected cut that actually looks as if it's combined with a burn—and that he's resumed bedwetting.'

'Fine,' Nina said, and Jack frowned.

'What does that mean?'

'You've already made up your mind.' She walked out of his office and to the nurses' station and set up her computer to input her notes—God, she was an angry thing, Jack thought. He felt like walking over and tapping her on the shoulder, telling her that, no, he hadn't made up his mind, that he was still trying to catch up on the notes, and that he didn't jump in with assumptions. He looked at all the facts and *then* he made up his mind.

So he started to.

He read the psychologist's notes though they dealt more with the issues surrounding the mother, and then he read Nina's.

They were incredibly detailed and her observations were astute, outlining how Tommy had first responded to her, that he had been precocious almost, sitting on her knee, playing with her lanyard, taking no direction from the father he knew, but in later visits he had turned more and more to his father, so much so that Nina had been about to close the case.

So what had gone wrong these last weeks?

Jack looked up and saw Nina tapping away on her laptop, then she stopped and yawned and gave her head a little shake. He watched as she stood and headed for the water cooler and then came back to the computer, frowning as she read through her notes. Then she must have hit 'send', because an update appeared in the notes Jack was reading.

And he read Nina's account of today.

She was a brilliant report writer. He had expected more passion, a little dig at the medial staff perhaps, but instead she had detailed all that had happened, and her conclusion that, given the injuries and the lack of any explanation, she had obtained an urgent court order that allowed supervised access only for the next seventy-two hours.

And Jack sat and racked his brains.

He shut out all chatter.

He was head of paeds for more reasons than his financial pull.

No one argument swayed him, no tearful plea prompted his signature on anything that he didn't believe in.

Jack walked over to the bedside where Nina now stood stroking Tommy's dark curls as he slept. 'Do you always get this involved?'

'Always.' She didn't look up. 'Right now my department is all this little guy's got.'

'As well as the medical staff.'

'I'm talking about family.' She looked up. 'He wants his father and I've been to court to stop that contact; it's not a decision that can be taken lightly. I have a worker booked for nine a.m. and she will supervise a visit, but really Tommy needs his father tonight.'

'I've been reading through the notes,' Jack said, only he didn't get to finish as he was interrupted by a sudden wail from a sleeping Tommy. Nina looked down, moved to comfort him as his eyes opened and he sat up, clearly terrified.

'It's okay, Tommy,' Nina said, sure the little boy was having a nightmare, but instead Jack told her to step out, already pressing the bell for assistance. He knew long before Nina did what was happening, because Tommy hadn't woken up. He was experiencing an aura, a sudden panic before a seizure, and Tommy nearly bolted from the bed as Jack firmly held him, then laid him back down as his body gave way to spasms...

Nina felt sick. There was no question now that she should go home and she headed to the office, watching as the nurses ran with the trolley, IVs were put up and drugs were given.

Yet nothing seemed to be working.

She heard the call go out for the anaesthetist and then she saw through a chink in the curtains that after only brief respite young Tommy's body was starting to seize again.

A grim-faced Jack came into the office a while later.

'He's anaesthetised and we're taking him down for an urgent head CT,' Jack told her. 'You need to let his father know.'

'What do I tell him?'

'Just tell him to get here,' Jack said. 'I'll be the one to tell him that it's not looking good.'

CHAPTER FOUR

IT WAS A wretched night.

She had to sit with a terrified Mike who arrived after Tommy had gone for his CT scan. Because of the court order, because of the possibility that he had caused the injuries, Mike would only be allowed to see Tommy supervised, and when Lorianna, the duty social worker, appeared in the waiting room to sit with him, although exhausted, the last thing Nina wanted to do was leave.

'Go home.' Lorianna pulled her aside. 'It's after one and you're due back at nine.'

'I want to hear the results.'

'They'll be the same results in the morning.' Lorianna was practical. 'Anything from dad?'

'Nothing.' Nina shook her head. 'I'd just spent the best part of an hour trying to convince Jack that Mike hadn't harmed Tommy and I've just heard a nurse saying that they're flagging brain trauma…' God, she was questioning herself, which Nina did often, but she had been so sure Mike hadn't hurt Tommy. The sight of the little boy seizing had really upset Nina and standing outside the CT area, seeing more and more staff rushing in, in a race to save a little life, had tears stinging her eyes.

'You need to go home.' Lorianna was firm. 'You know that.'

Nina did.

There would be another family or families that needed her tomorrow and it wasn't fair to them if she hadn't at least had some sleep, but it felt so wrong to be leaving, so terrible to just walk away, except Nina knew that she had to.

She said goodbye to Mike, told him she would be back first thing in the morning, and then headed out of the hospital building towards the street, where she would flag a taxi. Really, she should have called Security rather than walk in the hospital grounds this late at night, but right now she just wanted to get home. She questioned her decision, though, as a car slowed down beside her and she walked a little more briskly as the car kept pace with her and the window slid down.

'Can I give you a lift?'

Nina turned at the sound of Jack's voice and saw his luxurious Jag, along with his face. 'No, thanks.'

'I actually want to talk to you—it turns out that you were right.'

'Sorry?'

'Tommy hasn't got a head injury,' Jack explained. 'It's a nasty brain lesion that's been causing the seizures. I expect that's where his bruises and injuries are from. I just called in Alex Rodriguez, he's in there speaking with the father now...' He drove alongside as Nina walked on, her boots making a crunching noise on the icy sidewalk, her breath coming out in short white shallow bursts as she struggled to hold onto both her temper and her tears, but, oblivious, Jack spoke on. 'So there you go—we find out again that things are never as they seem. Nina, let me give you—' He never got to finish.

'"There you go!"' She swung around, biting back tired, angry tears. His car halted when she did and Nina said it again. '*"There you go?"* Is that all you have to say?' She should stop speaking now, Nina knew, should just run for the nearest cab, except she didn't. 'Are you telling me that Tommy has a brain tumour?' She was furious and let it show. '*"Oh, hey, Nina, I just thought you might like to know..."'*

'I'm trying to explain—'

'And doing an appalling job at it. Have you even listened to what I've told you? Have you any concept what that family's been through and now Tommy has a brain tumour? Do you expect me to do a little victory dance because I was right that Mike hadn't beaten him? Well, I won't because, unlike you, I don't take cheap shots.'

'Really?' Jack checked, thinking of her little dig about him reading that she had delivered just that morning. 'Or do you not even realise you're doing it?'

'At least I don't gloat over other's mistakes.'

'Now, hold on a minute...' Jack, rather illegally, parked the car in the hospital driveway and as he climbed out she stood there shaking with fury as several weeks of guilt and misery culminated in one very unprofessional row. 'What are you talking about?'

'You know full well what I'm talking about,' Nina shouted. 'Your little *I told you so* look when Baby Tanner was brought back in.'

'Baby Tanner?' She saw his nonplussed face, a frown marring his perfect features as he tried to recall.

'The eight-week-old my department discharged…' Guilt had lived with her since the night he'd been brought back and now, to add to her fury, Nina realised that he couldn't even recall the case. 'You don't even remember, do you?'

'Nina…'

'You really can't remember!' She was disgusted.

'Nina, what you fail to understand is…'

She didn't want to understand him, she didn't want to be inside Jack Carter's mind. She wanted him well away, and so with words she kept him well back. 'You're so bloody distant from your patients,' Nina shouted, 'you're so clinical and detached…' Her temper was nearing boiling point. It was two a.m., she was tired, cold and hungry and, despite herself, she fancied the arrogant man who stood in front of her, could see him so tall and groomed and just so sexy that she was perhaps more angry with herself than with him. 'You know what, Jack?' she hurled at him. 'You're burnt out.'

'Oh, I'm not burnt out, baby—I haven't even fired up…'

Baby! Of all the chauvinistic, unprofessional things to call her—to relegate her… And maybe he realised the inappropriateness of his comment, because he gave a small shake of his head before walking toward her. 'Get in the car.' He was so close she could smell him. 'I'll give you a lift.'

'I don't want a lift.'

'You're upset…'

Nina could hardly breathe she was so angry, so attracted and he was so terribly close. 'I'm more than angry,' Nina said, 'I'm ropeable.'

He had the audacity to smile.

'I'm sure it could be arranged.'

He smiled in the darkness and she could see his white teeth as they both held their breath. For a very long moment she thought he might kiss her, and wouldn't that be typical Jack Carter? Snog his way out of a row, dismiss any criticism with a stroke of his tongue.

She wanted him to, though, and that was what terrified her.

Her feelings for Jack actually terrified her. She simply didn't know how to react around him, didn't know how she felt.

Her eyes were savage now when they met his, as he again told her what she would do.

'I'm going to drive you home and we'll discuss this properly tomorrow.'

'There's nothing to discuss,' Nina said.

'Oh, I beg to differ...' Jack said, 'but not here, not now. Right now you need to calm down.'

He might as well have lit the match. He'd be telling her she was premenstrual next, which, as an aside, Nina realised in that dangerous flickering moment, she was.

But that wasn't the point.

That so wasn't the point.

'Oh, I'll calm down when I'm out of this place and as far away from you as I can get.'

'Nina...' He caught her coat as she turned to go, and swung her around.

'Is this off the record?' Nina checked.

'Of course!' Still, she was sure, there was an edge of a smile on his beautiful mouth.

'Screw you!'

She shook him off, walked noisily on as fast as she could without slipping on ice, which he would just love, Nina thought angrily. Wouldn't he just love watching her bottom up on the sidewalk as he slid past in his silver Jag?

She practically ran out of Angel's, hailed a cab and climbed in, cursing under her breath as he overtook them.

At the same time, a curse come from Jack too.

What the hell was all that about? Jack wondered as he headed for his apartment.

Drama he so did not need.

Yet…

He thought of her angry face, the stamp of her boots, the bundle of passion he'd just witnessed and had actually enjoyed. Jack winced a little as he recalled his own retorts, though, which were so unlike him. He didn't really row with anyone, didn't really discuss, he just told people how it would be.

Still, as he headed for home she soon disappeared from his mind. He was just mildly annoyed that he had dumped Monica that morning, because he could really use a decent unwind…

Detached, clinical, yep, Jack was guilty as charged.

But no.

Nina was wrong.

He was so not burnt out.

Walking into her apartment, Nina closed the door on the world and let out a very long breath.

She would not think about Jack.

Neither would she think about Tommy.

Quite simply, she *had* to sleep and had learnt long ago that sometimes you simply had to turn off fear and panic and just close your eyes for a little while.

But her hands were shaking as she poured a glass of milk.

Nina wandered through her apartment, hoping it would soothe her.

She had just moved in and it was *everything* to her. She'd fought for eight years to have this, a proper home where finally they could be a family.

She went first to Blake's room, looked at the mountain of boxes that would hopefully soon transform into a bed and bedside table and a chest of drawers, but so far the fairies hadn't been in to build them. She'd hopefully do that tomorrow night, or at the latest by Blake's access visit next weekend.

Then she moved to what would hopefully soon be Janey's bedroom, but instead of feeling soothed her chest tightened in fear when she thought about her sister.

Janey, even before their parents' death, had been a wilful, difficult child, but now at fifteen she was going spectacularly off the rails, and Nina was absolutely petrified for her younger sister.

She wanted Janey close and just hoped and prayed that the case meeting to be held in a few weeks would finally deem *her* a suitable guardian.

Nina had been seventeen when her parents had been killed in a horrific car crash. She had been considered old enough to look after herself, but too young to care for a one- and a seven-year-old and, she now conceded, the department had probably been right.

For two years she had been as difficult and as wild as Janey was now—worse, in fact. Devastated by the loss, not just of her parents but of her brother and sister too, Nina had been unable to keep up with the rent. She had lost her home and had spent a couple of years surfing friends' couches until finally she had found the pro bono centre, which had, quite simply, turned her life around. The people there had counselled her, offered support, both practical and financial, and she had commenced her studies at the age of nineteen and had qualified as a social worker at twenty-three.

But a junior social worker's wage had only allowed for a small one-bedroomed apartment and so she had still been unable to provide a proper home for her brother and sister, having to make do with just access visits and respite care.

Determined that they would be together Nina had scrimped and saved for the past two years, had gone without luxuries and every pay rise had gone towards her savings until finally she had found a three-bedroomed flat she could afford. Now, at the age of twenty-five, she was hoping that, after all these years, the Wilson siblings could be a real family.

But then she'd gone and lost her head with the Head of Paediatrics.

Nina tried to sleep.

Told herself that Jack wasn't going to have her fired—he'd been inappropriate too.

Terribly so.

She lay there in bed and thought of his words, star-

tled that just the repetition of them could have her body
aflame.

Nina turned over, screwed her eyes closed and did
her best not to think about him. She could not think
about Jack like that—except she was.

Her own thoughts startled her. She had never been
in a relationship, didn't know how to handle men un-
less she was dealing with them professionally.

She wasn't thinking professionally about Jack now.

And she hated sex, Nina reminded herself, except
she was thinking the sexiest thoughts now, and she
moaned out his name. For a breathless moment she
lay there, embarrassed and mortified for different reasons now at the thought that tomorrow she might have
to face him.

CHAPTER FIVE

IT ACTUALLY WASN'T an issue.

When Nina walked into ICU to check on Tommy, the sight of Mike's grief-stricken face was the only thing that consumed her and she barely noticed Jack speaking with Alex.

But Jack noticed her.

She was wearing a black skirt with a jade top and stockings and flat ankle boots today. She was far paler than yesterday and there were dark rings under her eyes, but even running on fatigue she was a ball of energy.

'How is he?'

Mike shrugged helplessly. 'He's just had some more tests and they're arranging a biopsy. They want to keep him on the ventilator for a few days...' He looked up at Nina. 'I'm so sorry for yesterday.'

'Let's deal with that another time,' Nina said.

'I think I was starting to realise that there was something really wrong with him... I just didn't want to know.'

'Mike, we'll go over all of that later. I've arranged a case meeting for tomorrow morning and we'll look at the supervised access order then, but right now let's just concentrate on Tommy.' Jack noted that she didn't ignore the issue of his outburst, there were just more important things to address right now. 'Have you rung your sister?' Nina asked. 'The one in Texas?'

Mike nodded. 'She's sorting out her children and flying out as soon as she can.'

'That's good.'

Jack had never been a particular fan of the social work department. Oh, he knew that they did a good job, but more often than not he found himself in contention with them. But today he saw that the holistic approach that had irked him so much was vital now.

Mike had no one, had lost his wife, his career and could possibly now lose his son, and he saw just how necessary it was that someone knew that there was a sister in Texas, that there was someone who knew that yesterday had been out of character for him.

He saw how important it was that when Mike was too emotionally distraught to speak that he had a voice, and in this case it came from Nina. He watched as her eyes skimmed past his face and landed on Alex's. 'If I liaise with your secretary, would you be able to attend a case meeting tomorrow?'

'We won't know much more by tomorrow,' Alex said.

'Sure, but I want to sort out the order and bring everyone up to speed,' Nina said.

Alex nodded and got back to the scan he was reviewing, but as Nina walked off Jack halted her.

'I'll catch up with you later, Nina.'

'Sorry?' She turned and frowned. 'You don't need

to be at the case meeting, it was the locum registrar who ordered the child abuse screen.'

'I'm aware of that,' Jack said. 'But I need to be brought up to speed on a few separate issues that arose last night.'

'Sure.'

Damn.

She had wondered how he would handle things—a letter from Admin perhaps, an internal email asking her to attend HR, or, and she'd rather hoped for this one, that her outburst would simply be ignored. Nina really couldn't believe she had spoken to anyone like that, let alone the Head of Paediatrics, Jack Carter himself! She had been completely unprofessional because, Nina knew, her feelings for Jack were completely unprofessional.

Of all the people to have a crush on...

How was it possible to be so attracted to someone that you actually didn't like?

It was a question that she couldn't answer and by three p.m., when her intercom buzzed and she was told Jack Carter was there to see her, Nina was actually relieved that soon things would be sorted out.

She just wanted this over with. 'Send him in.'

Nina took a deep breath, wondering if she should stand to greet him, if she should just apologise outright and explain how tired and emotional she had been yesterday.

She didn't get a chance to do either. The door knocked and as soon as she called for him to come in, he did so.

'You wanted to screw me?'

She had never considered that he might make her laugh, that he might have her smiling with his reference to her parting words last night.

'It's a figure of speech.'

'Oh!' He feigned disappointment. 'I shaved and everything. I even wore my best tie.'

He certainly had shaved, she'd noticed that this morning.

And, Nina reluctantly noted, he smelt fantastic.

He looked fantastic.

Jack would have had as little sleep last night as she'd had, yet there wasn't even a hint of weariness about him. Mind you, from what she had heard about him, Jack Carter was more than used to operating on minimal sleep. As well as his phenomenally busy job, his social life was daunting. If you lived in New York, you knew all about the Carters. They were glamorous, rich and had the social life to prove it. Jack was a regular feature in the social pages, a different woman on his arm each time, and more often than not witty little pieces written about the latest woman he had left in tears.

Nina didn't need to see it in magazines, there were many of his conquests dotted around the hospital, and the last thing she intended to be was another.

'I'd like to apologise for last night.' Nina wasn't as immediate in her apology as she had intended to be, but the fact that he had made her laugh a little made the words more genuine and a little easier to say. 'It came at the end of a very long day.'

'I understand that.' And if she had any hope that things would be left there, that her apology might suffice, then it was a very fleeting hope, because Jack was pulling up a chair. 'However, it does need to be addressed.'

'Really, it doesn't.'

'Really, it does.' He mimicked her voice and then he was serious. 'I'd like to offer an apology of my own—I shouldn't have told you that Tommy had a brain lesion the way that I did. I thought you would want to know before you went home last night.'

She was somewhat taken aback by his apology. 'How is he doing this afternoon?'

'He's still intubated and his father is with him. Alex is hoping the medication will start to really kick in and that his cerebral irritation will abate over the next forty-eight hours and then he can be extubated. They've taken a biopsy of the lesion.'

'Is it serious?'

'It's too early to say, though I would think that it is. Given the prolonged nature of his seizure, it sounds as if he's been having them for the last couple of weeks—that would explain the bruising and bedwetting. Still, the father has been negligent by not getting the cut and the bruises examined.'

'He was scared.'

'I'm aware of that, but his delay in seeking treatment for his son...' Jack didn't want to argue the point. 'But, yes, I accept that he was scared.'

'Well.' Nina gave him a brief smile. 'Thank you for stopping by and, again, I apologise for last night.' She stood, but Jack didn't.

'I haven't finished yet.'

'I've actually got quite a full workload...' Nina attempted, but could have kicked herself. He was Head of Paediatrics after all, and his diary would be full to bursting.

'Don't we all? But we're going to make some time to sit down and talk about Baby Tanner.'

'I'd rather not.'

'I didn't offer an option,' Jack said. 'And, yes, I'd love a coffee, thank you for offering.'

Reluctantly Nina headed over to her percolator. 'Cream and one sugar,' he called, and when she'd made him his drink and sat down, Jack immediately opened the conversation. 'I've had a look through the notes and it would seem I made a recommendation for Baby Tanner to be placed in foster-care.'

'You did.'

'But the social work department felt that the mother was doing well and with suitable provisions in place...' He gave her a wry smile. 'Does that sound familiar?'

'You don't remember him, do you?'

'A little bit, now that I've looked him up. What I don't understand is why you think that I'm supposed to remember him, why you're so upset.'

'I'm not.'

'I'd suggest you are.' Jack sat back in the chair, took a sip of his coffee as if he had all the time in the world. 'Last night it was clear that you're still furious about it, to the point where you were shouting in the hospital car park at the Head of Paediatrics, "Screw you!"'

'I've apologised for that.'

'And I've accepted your apology. I'm not here to discipline anyone. I'm simply here to find out why you are so upset with me about Baby Tanner.'

'It was what you said when he was readmitted…'
Nina shook her head, because that wasn't quite right.
'Or rather it was the look you gave.'

'The look?'

'The *I told you so* look.'

'I don't think so.' Jack shook his head.

'I remember it very well,' Nina said, and took a sip
of her own coffee.

'Was it this one?'

She looked over and almost choked on her mouthful of coffee.

Jack Carter was smiling at her and it was a smile
she had never seen. He was looking straight into her
eyes and his smile was wicked, triumphant. He held
that smile till her face was burning, till she had forced
herself to swallow the coffee she held in her mouth,
till she remembered again to breathe, because for a
moment there she had felt as if she were lying under
him, felt as she'd just found out what it was like to be
made love to by him.

'*That's* my *I told you so* look,' Jack said, and then
his face changed. His expression became serious, his
jaw tense, his eyes the same they had been the night
Baby Tanner had been brought in.

'What you saw was my *I hate this job sometimes,
why do people have children if they don't want them,
what the hell is wrong with the world that someone can
do this to an eight-week-old* look…'

'Oh.'

'They're two very different things and not for a minute was I blaming you for what had happened to Baby
Tanner.'

'Okay.'

'And it was the same look I gave you yesterday when you walked in and saw Tommy covered in bruises. Why would you think I blamed you?'

'People often do,' Nina answered tartly.

'Well, I don't,' Jack said. 'And I want to make that clear. There's no simple answer in a lot of these cases...' He would have spoken on but at that moment there was the sound of a commotion outside. The office door opened and Nina heard the receptionist shouting that Nina had someone in with her and that she simply couldn't go in—not that is made the slightest difference.

'Janey!' Nina stood. 'You can't just barge in here...'

'You said I could come by any time.'

Jack looked at the angry teenager who had just burst into the office, heard the challenge in her words, saw the anger in her stance, and decided the social work department really was the hidden front line of Angel's.

'I need some money,' Janey said. 'I haven't got any to ride the subway, and I'm hungry.'

'Wait outside and I will speak with you when I'm finished here.'

'I'm not waiting! Are you going to give me money or not?'

Jack frowned as Nina reached for her bag. 'Hold on a moment.' What on earth was she doing, giving this young woman money?

'Leave it, Jack.'

For a moment he did.

He watched as Nina handed over a few dollars, heard her tell Janey to be careful and that she would ring her later tonight. Then Nina asked her who she was with, where she was going, but all Janey had been interested in had been getting some money and, almost as soon as she had arrived, she left.

'I know I have absolutely no idea about the inner workings of the social work department,' Jack started, 'but I do not like the idea of angry, clearly troubled teenagers feeling they can just storm in here and demand—'

'She isn't a client,' Nina interrupted him. She sat back down at her desk and tried to keep her voice matter-of-fact as she explained to Jack what had just happened. 'Janey is my sister.'

'Your sister? So why is she...?' He never finished the question, realising even as he started to speak that it was none of his business anyway. Though that wasn't the reason that Jack stopped talking. It was because Nina had put her head in her hands and promptly burst into tears.

It wasn't a little weep either.

In that moment everything Nina was struggling with chose to finally catch up with her and she sobbed for more than a minute before attempting to pull herself together. When she did she was mortified that it was Jack who was there to witness her meltdown.

For weeks things had been building up. Janey's behaviour was getting worse and, given her job, Nina knew more than most that Janey was heading rapidly in the wrong direction, yet felt powerless to do anything.

'Please.' There were always tissues on her desk, usually for the clients, but Nina peeled off a generous handful and blew her nose. She couldn't bring herself to look at Jack. 'Can you leave?'

He just sat there.

'I don't want to discuss this.'

'Sorry, but you're going to.' Jack stood. 'But first I suggest—in fact, I insist—that you go home and get some sleep.'

'I can't go home.' Nina shook her head. 'It's impossible, I've got appointments, I need to—'

'You need to go home.'

And she gave in then as she truly was beyond exhausted. She had spent the weekend moving into her apartment, as well as arguing with Janey, as well as working at the pro bono centre in Harlem till late on Sunday, and yesterday had been impossibly long…

'Fine.'

'I'll drive you.'

'I can take the subway.'

'No.'

'I'll take a taxi.'

'I'm not going through this again,' Jack said. 'I'm not on call so I'm giving you a lift and this time you're not going to argue.' He rang down to Switchboard, told them he was out of range for the next forty minutes or so and then walked her out to his parking spot.

She could have taken a taxi, Jack knew that. He really didn't know why he was so insistent on driving her home himself. Rarely did tears move him and exhaustion was frequent in this place.

It was the complexity of her that had him unusually intrigued.

The traffic was busy but Jack negotiated it easily

and Nina was actually relieved for the lift, for the silence and warm comfort of his car, and grateful too that he didn't ask any questions.

'Just here,' she told him as they neared her apartment.

'I'll just park.'

'Just drop me here.' Nina was irritated. 'I really don't need to be seen to the door.'

'I'm a gentleman.'

Not from what she'd heard!

A delivery van moved off and Jack dived into the vacant space. Then he walked around the car and as she opened her door he held it for her, before locking the vehicle and walking beside her along the cold pavement.

'You're right,' Nina said as they climbed the stairs. 'I need to be home.'

'Go to bed,' Jack said. 'And I'll pick you up at eight, take you out for dinner.'

'I don't want dinner.'

'You don't eat?'

'I meant—'

'I know what you meant, but I'm not listening. I'm taking you out for dinner.'

'Because?'

'Because by eight o'clock. we'll both be hungry and,' Jack added, 'we never did get to finish our conversation.'

It was just dinner, Nina told herself as Jack walked

off, just dinner between two colleagues who had a few things that needed to be sorted out.

The stupid thing was she almost convinced herself that she meant it.

CHAPTER SIX

A GOOD SLEEP and a lot of talking to herself later, Nina sat opposite him.

He'd chosen the restaurant without consulting her, of course, and it was a really nice one. She knew that even before they were inside because someone opened the car door for her and then took Jack's car to be parked.

It was nothing Nina was used to and nothing she secretly coveted but, despite her values, despite everything she believed in, it was actually incredible to be taken somewhere so nice and, Nina reluctantly conceded as she glanced over at Jack, to be there with him.

He took a sip of the wine he had chosen and ordered after she had asked for a glass of house white and she smarted a bit at that—clearly he thought he knew better. Well, he did know better, Nina conceded as she took a sip too because it was fruity and light and probably fifty times more expensive than the one she would have chosen. But just as she almost started to relax, to believe that they were here to talk about work, Jack asked a very personal question. 'What's going on with your sister?'

'Why would I discuss that with you?'

'Because I happen to know a lot about teenagers.'

'I know quite a bit myself.'

'So you're dealing with this objectively, are you?' Jack checked. 'You're able to treat Janey as if she's a client at work.' He watched her tense swallow and conceded a brief pause. 'Let's order, and if you choose an omelette or a salad I'm going to override you and get the most expensive thing on the menu just to annoy you.'

'Well, can you get the most expensive vegetarian thing on the menu please?' She looked through the menu and... To hell with it, she was out with Jack Carter so she chose what she wanted—a tomato salad for a starter and then mushroom and goat cheese ravioli with saffron cream for the main course.

And, yes, maybe she could use a brain like his if it would help with her sister—she simply couldn't take the emotion out of the equation.

Jack could do it without blinking.

'My sister, Janey, is fifteen and my brother, Blake, is nine. They're both in foster-care—separate foster-homes...'

'So when you say that foster-care is no fairy-tale solution, you're not speaking just professionally?'

'No. Blake has been very lucky for the most part, but in the last year his placement hasn't been going so well. The couple he's with are getting old and their daughter has just returned from overseas with her children and I think they'd rather be spending time with them than Blake. He doesn't say much to me about it, I have him every alternate weekend, but I think he's spending an awful lot of time alone in his room.'

'And Janey?'

'Janey hasn't fared so well in the system. She was moved around a lot, but she's been with a woman, Barbara, for the last four years. In the last few months… I think Barbara's had about enough. Janey's skipping school, arguing, just delinquent behaviour…'

'What happened to your parents?'

'They died when I was seventeen,' Nina explained. 'I tried to get custody but…' She shook her head.

'Too young.'

'Yes,' Nina said, 'but it was a bit more than that. I was very angry at my parents for dying. I was a lot like Janey is now. I lost my temper with the social workers on more than one occasion.' It helped that he smiled a little as she told him, because the guilt of her handling of things back then still ate away at her to this day. 'So I managed to stuff everything up…'

'You were seventeen,' Jack pointed out. 'Do you really think you could have taken care of them?'

'No,' Nina admitted. 'But it just hurt so much that we were separated. My parents weren't well off, there was no insurance, no savings, nothing. I know the department was right to place them, but that was then and this is now. I've just moved into a three-bedroomed apartment and I'm about to go again and try for custody.'

'Without losing your temper this time?'

'Yes,' Nina said.

'Without getting all fired up.'

'Yes.' And this time she smiled.

'You're going to go in there being cool and the amazing professional that you are.'

'Thanks.' She looked over at him. 'It's hard enough

to be dispassionate when you're fighting for a client, but when it's family, well, you can imagine what that's like...'

Actually, Jack couldn't, but he chose not to say anything, just let Nina continue to talk. 'I thought there would be no problem, but Janey ran away a few weeks ago, and when she turned up on my doorstep I didn't let Barbara or the case worker know where she was. I know I should have rung straight away, I know I was wrong, but I just wanted some time to get to the bottom of what was going on before they took her back. Then the duty social worker turned up at my door and, of course, there she was.'

'Another black mark against Nina.'

'I just want my family together.'

'You'll get them.'

'I'm not sure.' She blew out a breath. 'I work very long hours...'

'Can you reduce them?'

Nina gave a tight shrug. She didn't want to drone on about her finances to someone who simply wouldn't understand. 'I also volunteer at the pro bono centre in Harlem eight hours a week...'

'Well, that can go,' Jack said, and Nina felt her hand tighten around her wine glass. She looked at him, at a man who had had everything handed to him on a plate as he coolly dismissed something that was very important to her.

'I happen to like working there,' Nina said. 'It's extremely important to me. Without them...' She stopped, she just wasn't going to get into this with Jack, but rather than letting her drop it Jack pushed for Nina to go on.

'Without them…?'

'They do amazing work,' Nina said. 'It's run by very passionate, caring people.'

'Unlike me.' Jack grinned. He could hear the barbs behind her words.

'I didn't say that.'

'You think it, though.'

Nina shrugged again.

'I can't afford to get involved, Nina.'

She didn't buy it.

'How can you not?' She blinked at him. 'You're a brilliant doctor. I've actually seen you in action the rare times you're hands on. You and I both know…' She halted. There were some things that should perhaps not be said.

'Go on,' Jack invited.

'I don't think I should.'

'Off the record?' Jack smiled. 'And, no, you can't screw me here.'

He made her blush, he made her smile, he gave her permission to be honest.

'I'm not criticising the other doctor, but I do think that had it been you who examined Tommy…' She took a slug of her wine before continuing. 'Well, things might have been picked up a little sooner.'

Jack would never criticise a colleague and certainly not to a woman he didn't really know—idle gossip was a dangerous thing—but he absolutely agreed with Nina. He'd thought exactly the same thing.

Not only that, he'd had a rather long and difficult

conversation with the locum registrar just that morning, not that he could share that with Nina.

'I just think...' She really should say no more, except his silence invited her to go on. Sometimes she was a little too honest and even as the words tumbled out, she wished she could take them back. 'Instead of sucking up to benefactors, you'd be better off with the patients.' She knew she had gone too far, knew from the flicker of darkness across his eyes that she'd overstepped the mark, and she recanted a little. 'Certainly the patients would be better off...'

She was nothing like Jack was used to.

Nothing like anyone he had ever been out with before.

He could not think of one person who had ever spoken to him like this, yet over and over she had.

'Do you ever got involved?' Nina asked a little later, when she was scraping her dessert bowl. 'I mean, do you ever get close?'

'Are we still talking about work?' Jack grinned.

'Of course.' Nina gave a tight smile. She already knew the answer in regard to his personal life. Jack saw the smile, matched it and then upped it, just looked at her and smiled till her face was pink and her toes were curling in her boots.

'No,' he said. 'And no at work as well.' Then he stopped smiling. 'I'm not a machine, Nina. I get a bit upset sometimes, I guess, and some things get to me more than others but, no, I work better by staying back...'

He thought he might get a brief lecture, thought the frown was a precursor to criticism, but then, perhaps properly for the first time that night, her eyes met his. 'You'd be really good at the pro bono centre.'

It was Jack frowning now. 'I already do a lot...'

'No.' She shook her head. 'I'm not asking you to volunteer. I'm just saying that someone like you would be really good.' She gave him a smile when he had expected a rebuff. 'I am sorry for what I said last night—I guess cool heads are needed at times.'

Except his head wasn't so cool now.

And, no, he never got involved on a personal level either. Jack didn't do *dating* and long conversations, and certainly no explorations into someone else's past, except he found himself wanting to know about a younger Nina, found himself asking how she'd fared when her parents had died.

'It was rough for a while, but I got there.'

'How?'

'I had friends.' She gave a tight shrug. 'Couch-surfed for a while...'

'Couch-surfed?'

'Slept on friends' sofas.' He watched her face burn and then blue eyes met his. 'I nearly ended up on the streets.'

Jack could perhaps see why she was so angry at times, why she struggled so much in her efforts to keep families together—given the impact it had had on her life when she'd lost hers. 'So how come—?'

'I'm not going there, Jack,' she interrupted.

'Sure,' Jack said. Usually it was him pulling back, usually it was him closing off and refusing to discuss things.

And so they chatted about other stuff when he really wanted to know more about Nina. He simply didn't know how to play her, because when he glanced at his phone and saw how late it was, had it been anyone else, they'd have been back at his apartment and safely in bed.

Safely in bed, because that was what Jack knew and did best. He wasn't used to that awkward moment when they climbed into his car, because usually both parties knew exactly where they were headed.

'No, thanks,' she said to his oh-so-casual offer of a nightcap at his place. 'It's already late and I'm the duty worker tomorrow night.'

So not only was Jack not used to going to back to *her place,* neither was he familiar with a smile at the front door and no invitation to come inside.

'Thanks so much for tonight,' Nina said. 'It was nice to clear the air.'

'Oh, we haven't cleared the air yet,' he said, and he gave her the kiss that he should have last night.

Not a gentle kiss, a very thorough kiss, a kiss that meant business.

She should have resisted, Nina thought as she kissed him back. She should have at least made some token protest, but there was something very consuming about being kissed by Jack, something that would make you a liar if you attempted to deny the effect, because like the man himself it was a top-notch kiss, and, like the man himself, very soon it went too far.

His mouth had left hers and had moved to her neck, his hands pulling her hips into him, and he was just as turned on as she was. He made sure Nina could feel it and then his voice was low in her ear. 'Am I going to be asked inside?'

'I don't think so.'

'Can you be persuaded?'

He kissed her again and, no, she couldn't be persuaded, because she trusted her heart to no one and certainly she'd be a fool to trust it to a man like Jack.

She pulled away. 'I'd better go.'

She was playing with fire here, Nina knew it. So she stepped back a little and went into her bag for her key.

'Nina—'

'Thanks so much for dinner.'

And she gave him a smile, stepped into the safety of her flat and closed the door on him. On them.

No matter how she might want to, Nina was so not going there.

These next few weeks were the most important of her life and she was not going into them with a head messed up by Jack Carter. And he would mess it up.

His reputation preceded him.

And she had her family to think of.

CHAPTER SEVEN

OVER THE FOLLOWING days Nina avoided Jack. She didn't return his calls and when he stopped her in the corridor one lunchtime and asked if she wanted to go out that night, she gave a vague reason as to why she couldn't, was polite and smiled and then quickly moved on.

Unused to being rebuffed, Jack didn't like it one bit.

Still, even if he had to face her in a few moments, right now there were more important things on his mind. Jack, Alex and the oncologist Terence were going over the planned course of treatment before speaking with Mike, and on one thing Alex remained resolute.

'I want it made clear to the father that there are no guarantees. I don't want him to be given false hope. Really, we're just trying to buy Tommy some more time here, because even if the chemo does shrink it, I don't know that surgery will be an option. It would be incredibly risky—most surgeons wouldn't touch it.'

'But you take on patients that others wouldn't,' Jack pointed out. 'That's why Angel's needs you.'

They stopped the discussion as there was a knock on the door, but Jack knew full well what was getting to Alex. Still, he wasn't going to discuss it in front of

Terence, and now the oncology nurse had arrived to sit in on the discussion with Mike.

'The father's outside with the case worker,' Gina said.

'Okay.' Jack nodded. 'Tell them to come in.'

Nina didn't blush when she saw him, Jack noted, and, yes, her coolness towards him was grating, her dismissal when he called or spoke to her seriously irked him—perhaps because he wasn't in the least used to it. Still, right now the focus of the meeting was Tommy and his father and preparing them for the difficult months ahead.

'It's basically a marathon that we're asking you to run,' Terence explained. 'It's an aggressive tumour and we're hoping to reduce it, but it's not going to be easy...'

'We're up for it,' Mike insisted.

'We need you fully on board,' Terence reiterated a little while later, because Mike just kept nodding at what ever was said. 'Any bruising or bleeding, a raised temperature, even a cold and Tommy is to be seen urgently.'

'Of course.' Mike sounded annoyed and it was then that Jack cut in.

'You need to listen to this carefully.' Jack was firm. 'Last week you were hiding Tommy's injuries from the hospital.'

'I didn't know what was happening,' Mike admitted. 'I thought you were out to take him away from me.'

'Well, we're not,' Jack said. 'Tommy needs you now more than ever, but we are all going to have to start trusting each other and being honest each with each other, and I'm telling you straight up that I will not accept any outbursts with my staff like the one I witnessed last week, no matter how emotional things get.'

'There won't be any more outbursts,' Mike said, and he looked at Nina. 'I've apologised to Nina, and I apologise again.'

'Mike's going to do the men's anger and emotion course that the pro bono centre runs,' Nina said. 'Aside from what happened in Emergency, I think it will be very helpful for Mike to have that resource in the months ahead.'

And on the meeting went. Terence had to get back to the ward but Mike had more questions.

'But if the chemo works, surgery might get rid of it.'

'It's a possible option,' Alex said carefully, 'but the lesion is in an exceptionally difficult location.'

'Have you done surgery like this before?'

'I've done similar,' Alex said, and Jack stepped in.

'Each case is unique.' He was as calm as always, Nina noted, and, she conceded, sometimes it was a good thing, because the emotion in the room was palpable. 'Each case is continually assessed. We'll know more once we see how Tommy responds to the chemotherapy.'

'But—'

'We're going to do our best for your son,' Jack said, 'but it would be wrong of us to say that this is a straightforward case—it's incredibly complicated. However, you do have the best team and the best resources available to your son. That much I can guarantee you.'

Mike nodded, stood when Alex did and shook his hand.

'Right.' Nina stood too once Alex had left. 'I'll take you up to the oncology ward and show you around.'

'I can do that,' Gina said. 'I'm going there now and I want to go over some of the side effects of the medication with dad.' She smiled at Mike. 'It will be good for Tommy if you're already familiar with the place when we bring him over.'

Which left Nina alone with Jack.

'You've been avoiding me.'

'I haven't,' Nina lied. 'I've just been busy.'

'Well, after work tonight…'

'I'm working at the pro bono centre,' Nina said quickly.

'If you'd let me finish,' Jack said, 'I was going to ask if I could speak with you after work about the pro bono centre—I was hoping to find out some more about it.'

Liar, Nina thought, but she was in no position to refuse him. Someone with Jack's skills would be an amazing coup for the pro bono centre, but she didn't like being manipulated and certainly she wasn't going to go through another dinner with him, or another kiss goodnight, because she knew full well what might happen. So she smiled sweetly back at him, played along with his game, but on her terms.

'Come and watch tonight,' Nina said. 'I'm running a clinic—it might give you a feel for the place.'

'Great!' Jack grinned through gritted teeth, because he'd been hoping to discuss things over a nice bottle of champagne. 'I'll pick you up—'

'I'll meet you there,' Nina broke in. 'My clinic starts at seven.'

'See you there then!' Jack said. 'What time does it finish?'

'About nine, nine-thirty.'

His smile only left his face when she was out of the office. A night at some pro bono centre was something he so did not need, but it would be worth it, Jack decided.

He'd have her in bed by ten.

She hadn't changed, Jack noted, because she had on the same purple stockings and a jumper that she'd been wearing earlier. He stood outside the pro bono centre and as she walked towards him he realised that her entire work wardrobe consisted of a black skirt, a grey skirt, a grey pinafore and then stockings and jumpers of various shades.

He wanted to take her shopping.

He wanted to spoil her, which was a first for Jack.

Oh, he was a generous date and lover. He had both a boutique florist and jeweller on speed dial and had tabs at the smartest bars and restaurant, but somehow with Nina he knew that wouldn't impress her.

And he wanted to.

'You're probably going to be bored,' Nina warned. 'I really deal mainly with paperwork, helping people with social security forms and housing and benefits and things.'

Jack had done a lot of work for charity, but had never actually worked for one. He really had no idea what to expect, a sort of massive soup kitchen perhaps, but he was surprised at the modern offices and the air of organisation.

'There's a doctors' clinic on tonight as well,' Nina explained. 'They're held alternate nights.'

'Well, while I'm here…' Jack said, more than happy to pitch in, but Nina shook her head.

'Sorry. You have to formally apply, your references and registration need to be verified, insurance…' She looked at him. 'It's not a back-street organisation, it's a non-profit organisation with some salaried staff and an awful lot of volunteers.' She gave him a smile. 'You can sit in with me if you like.' She saw his eyebrows arch. 'Though I'll have to ask each client if they mind you being present.'

It was like being a medical student again and Jack felt a surge of irritation. Every minute of his day was accounted for, and now, when he could really help, he was forced to take a back seat instead.

Literally.

He sat in an office as client after client came in.

Nina would explain to each of them that Jack was a senior paediatrician and there to observe, and that he was, hopefully, considering joining the centre. Most smiled and thanked him.

For sitting there.

Some asked that he wait outside.

Nancy gave him a very suspicious look but agreed that he could stay. She was an exhausted-looking lady with a nasty scar over one eye and a nose that had been broken and not reset.

'Where are the little ones?' Nina asked.

'Steven's home and watching them,' Nancy said. 'He's doing good now, much more sensible.'

'How was court?' Nina asked.

'I'm here,' Nancy said. 'No conviction recorded.'

'That's great,' Nina encouraged.

'I'm so grateful. I don't know what I was thinking back then.'

'Four children to feed maybe?' Nina said.

'Nancy left a violent household with her children,' Nina explained. 'They were on the streets for a while and Nancy got arrested for shoplifting. It was then that she was referred to us and we arranged emergency shelter. Nancy has found employment since then, but a conviction would have threatened that. She was represented by one of the centre's lawyers…' And Jack listened and heard how in the year since she'd left home Nancy really had turned her life around. She was out of emergency housing now and in rental accommodation and her eldest son, Steven, was finally attending school and taking it seriously. Nina was going through some welfare forms with her now that her circumstances had changed. 'Things are looking a lot better.'

'They are.' Nancy nodded.

'Now…' As the appointment concluded Nina smiled. 'Do you remember I spoke to you about Dr Cavel?'

'The cosmetic surgeon?'

Jack's ears really did pick up. If they were talking about Louis Cavel, he was renowned, so renowned that he had done some rather impressive work on Jack's own mother.

'We had a meeting a few weeks ago and I mentioned you to him, as I said I would. He had a look at your photos and he really thinks he can help.' Jack watched as Nancy started to cry and Nina went from her chair and put her arms around the woman. 'He's really looking forward to meeting with you.'

'The truth?' Nancy checked.

'Absolutely,' Nina said.

'I'm so ashamed of my face,' Nancy sobbed. 'I feel people looking at my scars all the time and every time I look in the mirror I remember what he did.'

'Dr Cavel gets that. He wants to help you move on and really put this behind you,' Nina said. 'We're all so proud of the effort you've made this past year.'

'This is the sweet reward.'

'I believe so.' Nina said. 'I've heard that his work is second to none. Now…' Nina stood and went through the file and handed Nancy a business card '…he is holding a clinic here on Thursday. It's strictly by appointment, the wait for him is huge, but he does want to see you, so I've scheduled one. Can you get here on Thursday?'

'Oh, I'll be here.' Despite her tears a huge smile split Nancy's face. 'I wouldn't miss it. I never thought I'd be getting my face fixed.'

'I can't wait to see you when you do.'

As Nancy left, Nina turned at Jack's voice.

'We are talking about *the* Louis Cavel?'

'He donates fifteen hours a month,' Nina said. 'And the difference he makes to lives is amazing. Nancy is already a changed woman, but just wait till she's got rid of those scars, she'll be unstoppable.' She smiled at Jack. 'Louis loves the work he does here—he says it grounds him after dealing with rich socialites who have nothing more to worry about than new crows' feet appearing…'

'He's my mother's cosmetic surgeon.'

Her lack of embarrassment at her faux pas was refreshing, and when she laughed, so did Jack.

'So what will he do for Nancy?'

'A miracle,' Nina said. 'I had a woman last year who had massive, ke-, ke-, I can't remember the name. Really thick scars.'

'Keilod scars,' Jack said.

'That's it, and her nose had been broken numerous times. Louis did the most amazing work, he always does—he gives these women their faces back.'

As the evening progressed Jack was far from bored.

He was, in fact, fascinated.

They didn't finish till after ten, not because of clients but because they actually sat talking and Jack became more and more impressed with what he'd never thought he would be. He started to understand the holistic approach that she favoured so much, and they carried on chatting as Jack drove her home.

'We offer counselling not just to the women and children but also their partners. Some women stay and some men do choose to change.' She saw his disbelieving eye-roll. 'Some do!'

'Perhaps,' Jack said, though he'd have to see it to believe it.

Actually, he wanted to see it to believe it.

'I've got a fundraiser for the burns unit next weekend.' Jack glanced at her. 'Come with me.'

'I don't think so.'

'No, please. You dismiss all the work that I do, just as I dismissed yours, and I would like you to see what I do.'

'Jack…' Her voice was slightly weary. 'I'd stick out like a sore thumb at one of those dos.'

'I can—'

'Please,' Nina broke in. 'Don't offend me by offering to buy me something to wear. If I was a millionaire I still wouldn't drop a thousand dollars on an evening dress and shoes.'

A thousand dollars wouldn't begin to cover it and Jack felt that knot of unease again in his stomach as he thought of the wealth that surrounded him, the money that made money and the games that he played.

'Think about it.'

'Maybe.'

She wouldn't.

'And speaking of men who don't change—' they were nearing the turn-off for her apartment and Jack wanted to drive on '—would you like dinner?'

'I had something to eat at work.'

'A drink perhaps?'

This question Nina did think about, she really did.

She sat with her bottom being warmed on a leather seat and glanced over at him, at his perfect profile. Then, as his hand moved to turn on the music, she saw his manicured nails and the flash of his expensive watch and she remembered that he was everything she abhorred, except still she wanted him.

And Jack was the first man she had ever wanted.

The first.

Avoiding him hadn't cleared her head—her mind was still full of him. The fight to concentrate on anything but him was a permanent one these days and she knew nothing would come of it, knew it would be short-lived, but there were too many less–than-pleasant memories in her head, and Nina wanted a nicer one to replace them.

And so she agreed to a drink.

'Please.'

He had been sure she'd refuse him, and just as he blinked at her acceptance she surprised him again.

'Maybe we could have a drink back at your place.'

It was like a game with two players and they were both assessing the rules.

She walked into his gleaming bachelor pad and Jack Carter was everything she wasn't into.

Not just wealth-wise either.

He undid her coat with this half-smile on his face, made a lot of work of her belt, and that made her tingle in places she shouldn't.

It was a tiny thing, but Nina felt her heart beating in her throat.

'Drink…' Jack said, pouring her one without waiting for her reply.

He watched her at the window, still in her boots and that awful grey pinafore, but, he conceded, he liked the purple.

But it wasn't just her appearance that was different from that of any woman he usually brought home, it wasn't just that Nina was different.

He actually *felt* different.

Very different.

He just couldn't nail why.

He took off his tie, kicked off his shoes, took a seat on a low lounge and watched as she stood there, looking out at the New York skyline she loved.

'What are you thinking?' Jack asked.

'Nothing. I'm just looking at the view.'

'Come on, Nina, what are you thinking?'

Nina turned. 'Will I be sent to the naughty corner if I don't tell you?'

'Blindfolded.' Jack actually laughed.

'I don't think I like you, Jack.' It was strange she could be so honest, could turn and look him in the eye and say exactly what she thought. 'And I know this isn't going anywhere.'

'Why not?'

'Oh, please,' she scoffed. She didn't need the sweet talk, she really didn't and told him so as she walked over to where he sat. 'I don't know that I'm up for the sexual marathon of the next few days or weeks and then the awkwardness after...'

'I'm never awkward,' Jack said, and watched as she smiled. 'I bet you like really considerate, thoughtful lovers who say, "Is this okay for you, Nina?" as you lie there bored out of your mind.'

'No.'

He frowned.

'So, if you're not sure you like me, why are you here?'

'Maybe for the same reason as you.'

'I'll tell you why I'm here.' And she waited for that beautiful mouth to tell her the reason, for him to say something crude perhaps, yet it was he now who surprised her. 'Unlike you, I happen to know that I like the person I've recently been spending time with. Admittedly, that's taken me by surprise—no offence, but you're not my type.'

'None taken,' Nina said, 'because you are *so* not mine.'

'However...' he was looking at her mouth as he spoke, his hands sliding up between her thighs 'I... think the sex could be amazing, and I actually have no idea where we are going and no idea where this is leading, just that I would like to get to know you some more.'

He was still looking at her mouth.

'I should warn you, though.' He smiled as he did so. 'Those touchy-feely, sensitive new-age lovers you're used to? I'm going to ruin you for ever...'

'Jack, you don't know me at all—there haven't been any sensitive new-age lovers, as you call them. I've never been in a relationship.'

She felt his hand still on her thigh, smiled at the flare of shock and panic in his eyes.

'I'm not a virgin.' Nina couldn't help but laugh at his reaction.

'Thank God for that.' Jack blew out a breath. 'Never?'

'Never,' Nina said. 'I don't really have time.' And she certainly had no intention of telling him about her past or admit to Jack that he was the first man she'd been attracted to in the longest, longest time... ever, really. That the nights spent on friends' sofas had rather too often had a down side in the shape of her friends' brothers or fathers—no, Jack didn't need to know all that.

It was far easier to let him think this was just casual, even if she'd never wanted anything like this in her life before. So that was what she told him, that just for tonight was completely fine. And Jack told himself that he could deal with this. After all, he'd never been in much of a relationship either, but there was a certain disquiet at her honesty that she was only there for sex. Jack noted his own double standards and got over them quickly, his hand resuming its path on her thigh.

If she had thought he would haul her over his shoulder and throw her onto the bed she couldn't have been more wrong. If she had thought he might quickly undress her, she had it wrong there too, because instead he kissed her.

A kiss that was far more tender than expected, a nice kiss that turned into a deeper kiss, but really, though, his kiss was measured and thoughtful and the hand on the back of her head was not bold or forceful, it was the other hand that misbehaved.

It climbed up her stockings, without even pretending to idle, and he stroked her through her pantyhose. He pushed where he could not enter, he fiddled and he probed and he stroked her as, like a gentleman, he kissed her.

And she kissed him back and wriggled on his knee until she could not stand the tease, couldn't take the frustration any more.

'Tear them…' she breathed into his mouth.

He ignored her.

'Jack…' She pulled her mouth away. 'Tear them.'

'No.' His whole hand cupped her. 'Because I like them and I lied, it will be awkward when I see you in these stocking at work…'

'I've got loads.' But he kept stroking her and kissing her till she wanted to climb off his lap and take the bloody things off herself, except he pulled her down harder to him. She wanted him to undress her, wanted him to take her to bed, wanted to catch her breath, but he did not let her. Jack just kept touching her through her stockings and kissing her, because with his hand working its magic a kiss was all it would take to undo her. And he did not give in even when she tried to move a little to undress him to reciprocate.

'Why are you so stubborn?' Jack said when she held onto her orgasm.

'I'm not.' She could hardly get her breath, yet she refused to just give in to him. She didn't know why she was fighting it, she just didn't want to let go.

She wanted him to let her down, wanted him to be selfish, wanted to fault him in some way so that she could get him out of her mind, but she was failing miserably as she bit her lip, desperately trying not to come. He felt her thighs clamp around his hand, felt her breath rapid in his mouth and he stopped stroking, just enjoyed the small jolts of her body and the triumph of beating her resistance, but more than that, her reluctant pleasure was his.

He angered her.

She didn't know why.

Maybe it was the combination of good looks and wealth and knowing that things came so easily to him.

Even her.

That he simply knew he was that good made her angry and she turned on his lap to face him and refused to simply hand over control, to just lie there when he took her and whimper his name.

So, facing Jack, she kissed him, a different kiss this time. He was detained at her pleasure now, so it was the buttons to his shirt that she opened. He moved her hips up just a little higher so that his erection pressed into her and she kissed down his face to his neck, trying to gauge his collar line, nipping his neck just a little lower and sucking hard. There was a fight for control here and one Jack wasn't used to, but he was up for it, and their mouths found each other as she tackled his belt.

And she didn't just find out what sort of a lover Jack was, Nina found out what sort of a lover she could be.

That she could demand and be met, that she could offer no explanation but be understood. She unbuckled his belt and the top button of his trousers too, freeing him, and he let her feel a lot of him, then his hand moved in and shredded her stockings and her panties too, and she moaned with the pleasure of his fingers inside her and his mouth on her neck, and then somehow Jack made even the search for a condom sexy.

'I've got a little job for you.'

She had to lean over to his discarded jacket, had to find the little silver packet while his other hand stroked her bum, and then she had to rest back on her booted heels with his huge erection between them.

'Here.' She held out the packet.

'I'm busy,' he said, trying to find the zipper to her dress. 'You put it on.'

'You're old enough to dress yourself, Jack.' And she stayed back on her heels and held him, stroked him upwards over and over with both hands, one after the other in an endless tunnel till Jack was the one holding on now, Jack was the one fighting not to come.

'Why are you so stubborn, Jack?' Nina teased.

'Why are you?' Jack said, and lifted her hips enough so that she was over him, till her hands were removed from him and she had to steady herself on his shoulders. Then his hands held her hips and he pulled her down just a little way, just enough to teach her a very hard lesson, and then he lifted her a little and he watched her face as he did it again, and it was then that Nina conceded these were dangerous, reckless games and she never played them, but it was very easy to lose your head around Jack.

He watched as she went to retrieve the packet, but Jack changed his mind.

He didn't want sex on the sofa and neither did he want to be driving her home at two a.m. or calling a taxi, which he was somehow sure that she'd demand, because, unlike others, Nina didn't seem to want an entry pass to his bedroom. Nina wasn't even attempting that futile entry into his heart.

This, it would seem, was all she wanted.

It was Jack, as he kissed her into the bedroom, who wanted more.

He took off her dress in one motion.

And off came the purple jumper too and he looked at the tattiest bra he'd ever seen, and he even made her laugh as he took it off.

'Dressing to impress, Nina?'

'I don't need to.'

She didn't, because never had Jack cared less about the packaging. All Jack wanted was what was inside, but still she resisted.

Not with her body.

Her mouth met his as she undressed him. Nina indulged herself, because he was easily the most beautiful man she had ever seen, or had felt beneath her fingers. He was as luxurious naked as he was dressed. He smelt like Jack but a close-up version that she got to taste, and he acted like Jack, but a more intimate version that she now got to sample.

But, yes, she resisted, because even with Jack inside her, even with her body flaring with heat as he moved deep within her, even while being given the full Jack Carter experience, she held back just one vital piece, and he knew it.

'Nina…' He was chasing something and he didn't know what it was. He could feel her wanton beneath him, every lift of her hips bringing him closer. Her mouth was as probing as his, on his neck on his shoulders, her fingers scratching his back. It was the best sex he could remember, but he wanted something more. She was moaning beneath him and he guided her towards freefall, except he was used to more cheering from the stands, for the chant of his name or shouts of approval, for a giddy declaration as he hit the mark. He didn't need it and never had he actually wanted it, but as she throbbed beneath him, as he gave in to the sheer pleasure, Jack still wanted more.

His tongue was cool when he kissed her afterwards and she lay there, catching her breath for a very suitable while.

So now she knew just how good sex could be and all it did was confuse her, because she just couldn't imagine feeling like this with another man. She looked at Jack and he looked at her and Nina had to be very sure that she held onto her heart, but he had no idea of the gift he'd just given her. Even if soon he'd move on from her.

No idea at all.

'I'm going to get a taxi…'

He almost laughed.

A black laugh perhaps, because how many times had he lain in this very bed, wishing he could hear those words rather than have to do the conversation thing in the morning?

And now he had them from the one woman he didn't want to hear them from.

'You're not getting a taxi, your clothes are all torn…' Jack said. 'I'm not putting you in a taxi with no underwear on.'

'Drive me, then.'

'I will,' Jack said, and pulled her over to him. 'In the morning.'

Most mornings he woke up feeling somewhat stifled, an arm draped around him, or fingers running up his back, or, worse, the smell of breakfast and the sound of talking, except when he woke at six the next morning, Nina was exactly where she'd removed herself about two minutes after he'd pulled her over towards him.

Curled up on the edge of the bed and facing away from him.

CHAPTER EIGHT

IT ACTUALLY WASN'T awkward when Nina saw Jack at work.

She was too busy.

She was allocated several new families and as the days passed her paperwork piled up, but there was always somewhere else she needed to be.

'How are you doing?' She smiled at Tommy, who was looking so much better than he had on admission. The oncology nurse Gina was adding something to his IV and smiled at Nina. The medication had, for now, stopped the seizures and there was some colour in his cheeks, though it wouldn't be for long. Tommy was starting chemotherapy on Monday and from what she had heard it was going to be especially gruelling.

'Good,' Tommy said, and then introduced her to the woman sitting by his bed. 'This is my aunt, she's staying for the weekend.'

'I'm Kelly.' Tommy's aunt smiled. 'I'll be coming back as often as I can. Mike's got a job interview today, but he's coming in this afternoon.'

'That's good.'

It was awful.

Nina couldn't believe how hard it was for this family, couldn't fathom having to look for a job when your child was so sick. She was trying to arrange some accommodation for Mike nearer the hospital for the times Tommy would be here during his treatments, but there was only so much she could do and as she said her goodbyes and walked off, Gina voiced what she was thinking.

'Cruel, isn't it?'

Nina nodded. 'I'm going to look into it all again—see if there is anything more the department can do.'

'The poor man's trying to be in five different places at once, and the only place he wants to be is here with his son.' Gina sighed and when Nina got back to her office she sat with her head in her hands for a moment, because she'd added mandatory counselling to the list of places where Mike needed to be.

And again she questioned herself.

Still, she couldn't dwell on it for too long as she needed to add an urgent addendum to her report for court the next day.

Jack had rung a few times but she'd kept it short, had told him she was snowed under with work, had done everything to not give in to the urge to repeat things with him.

Yes, she had enough to contend with and it wasn't going to get easier any time soon, Nina thought as an angry Janey landed in her office at four p.m., after school, sulking, angry and confused about why Nina now had the three-bedroomed apartment but they still hadn't moved in with her.

'I've applied to be guardian for both you and Blake

and the department has to come and inspect the flat and check everything thoroughly.'

'Yeah, well, I don't believe you,' Janey shouted when Nina told her that she'd put the application in as soon as she'd secured the apartment. 'If you really wanted us, you'd have had us living with you years ago.'

Janey used words like knives and hurled them at Nina regularly, but though Nina had learnt to deflect most of them, these were the ones that hurt the most, because it killed her that she hadn't been able to keep her family together.

'It's not that straightforward, Janey.' Nina did her best to stay calm. 'And it's not fair to Barbara either, for me to just—'

'Barbara's a cow!' Janey huffed.

'I don't like you speaking like that.'

'Well, she is.'

Nina gritted her teeth and not for the first time questioned if she was up to the job of dealing with such an angry teenager. Of course, professionally she was but, as she often said to tearful parents who sat in this office and asked how she handled things so well, she got a break from it, got to go home at the end of each day. If things went well, in a few weeks she could be fully responsible for Janey, and what scared Nina the most was that if she wasn't up to the job, Janey's bad behaviour would escalate.

'Things are moving forward,' Nina said. 'I know it seems to be taking ages but I haven't been in the apartment long. Why don't we go and get something to eat and I'll show the photos I've taken? I've got all the furniture now for your room.'

'I thought you were working.'

'I'm going to be working till late,' Nina said, 'so I can take a break now.'

They took the lift and there were several choices where they could eat—there were a few cafés in the hospital so that parents could come and share a meal with their child if they were able to, or to spend some time away from the bedside with siblings and such. The whole hospital was geared to being not just child friendly but family friendly, but Nina was starting to feel as if her dream of her family being together was fading before it even had a chance to take off. Maybe they'd do better just walking.

'What do you want to eat?'

She was met with Janey's shrug.

They settled for the coffee bar and took a seat at the back where it was a quiet enough to talk. Nina bought Janey her favourite muffin and frappe and herself a regular coffee, deciding she wasn't hungry yet and would get something to eat later.

'Here.'

Should it annoy her that Janey didn't bother to say thank you? Should she let the small things go?

No.

She thought of their parents, how they'd insisted on good manners, but if she said anything, Janey would simply get up and walk out, and not wanting to risk that she let it go.

'I am doing my best.'

'Whatever.'

'I've got Blake this weekend,' Nina said. 'Why don't you come?'

Janey didn't answer. Nina quietly thought that Janey might very well be jealous of the more structured access Nina had with Blake, but that was because of his age and the distance he lived from Nina, which made shorter visits impossible. With Janey it was mainly holidays and the occasional sleepover, especially as Janey's weekends were taken up with sport activities.

'I could take you to netball.'

'I'm not doing netball any more.'

'How come?' Nina asked. 'You loved it, Blake and I were going to come and watch.'

'Yeah, well, don't bother. I got dropped.'

'How come?' Nina pushed. 'You were doing really well.'

'Till I swore at the umpire.' Janey was peeling apart her muffin, not looking at Nina as she spoke. 'And Barbara says that if I'm going to carry on like that then I can spend the weekend sorting out the basement.' She looked up at Nina. 'I guess if you ring her, though, she might let me come…'

'No.' Nina did her best not to be manipulated. Barbara was doing the hard yards, dealing with Janey, and Nina simply refused to interfere in the groundings and early bedtimes Barbara was trying to rein Janey in with. 'Barbara's right not to just let it go. Janey, you loved your netball. What were you doing, swearing at the umpire?'

'She was a stupid cow.'

'Everyone's a cow to you…' Nina tried to hold onto her temper, tried not to upset Janey, but it was impossible. She had no real authority with her sister. Janey pulled all the strings and she started pulling them now.

'Yeah, well, you're the biggest cow.' Janey stood. 'I'm stuck cleaning out a basement all weekend while you're busy spoiling Blake. Thanks a lot, sis...'

And she stormed out of the café and straight past Jack, not that she noticed him.

Jack noticed her, though.

He moved out of the way as a fast-moving, angry teenager stormed past and he looked into the café and saw Nina resting her head on her hands. He wanted to go over to see if she was okay but he'd just been called for a consult in ICU so he'd make time for Nina later.

And he would.

Jack was determined now, because he could not, *could not*, stop thinking about her.

It was an absolute first for him.

Jack's days were too busy to spend time dwelling on one woman, but he woke up thinking of Nina, spent the day with her sort of present in his mind. And the evenings were impossible, because she was *always* busy and sometimes she didn't even return his phone calls.

Another first.

So when he rang at seven that night only to find out that she was working late and didn't have time to stop, like some idiot he found himself walking through a dark social work department to the light from under her office door with a bottle of sparking water and some take-out.

'Jack, I really can't stop.'

'You can't eat?'

He had a good point. That coffee with Janey had been a long time ago, but it wasn't just the timing that was the problem. She was used to Jack looking completely gorgeous and groomed at all times, but she was slightly disarmed at the sight of him in scrubs—he was displaying rather more skin than she could deal with and say no to, so she kept her voice matter-of-fact as she declined him.

'I can eat, but I have to work. I'm due in court in the morning and I have to finish this report…'

'You haven't got five minutes?'

And she remembered her own manners, or she got the delicious waft of food, or it could have been that Jack was someone she found it incredibly hard to say no to, but she gave him a smile and gave in. 'Thank you.'

'How was your day?'

'Busy,' Nina said. 'How was yours?'

'Full on…' He chatted as he served up their meals. 'I've spent most of it up in ICU. There's a little one giving the paed team a headache. Still, we've got her stable now and a plan for tomorrow.'

'Sounds good.' It didn't annoy her any more that he never really used patients' names.

'And there's been progress in other areas,' Jack continued. 'We got the go-ahead on the supervised waiting room.'

'That's going to be so well utilised.' Nina took a forkful of noodles and they were utterly delicious. 'I can't think of the times I've wanted to speak to a parent away from the family, to be able to have the children looked after, even for a little while…'

'It was the one thing the ER nurses really wanted, so it will be good to get it off the ground. So, what have you been up to?'

'Just work,' Nina said.

'How are your brother and sister?'

'Pretty much the same.'

She was nothing like anyone he'd ever dated. Usually it was the woman trying to get Jack to open up or to tease out information from him. He knew full well that Janey had upset her today and yet Nina simply wouldn't share it, and it infuriated him as he swallowed a taste of his own medicine.

They chatted some more about work and Nina finished her food and thanked him for stopping by, but Jack didn't move from the chair he was sitting on.

'Jack, I really need to work.'

'I won't interrupt.'

He sat quietly as she typed and Jack drank sparkling water till his patience waned.

'What's the report about?' Jack asked.

'It's not one of your patients.'

Still he sat there.

Still she worked.

'Tell you what.'

Nina rolled her eyes as Jack interrupted her again.

'Why don't you come back to my place when you're finished?'

'Because I have to go home. I need to wear a suit for court in the morning.'

And he really wanted to see her in a suit! 'Tell you what, give me your keys and I'll go back to your place…'

'Excuse me?' She had no idea the concession he was making, how he never went to a woman's place. Jack liked to be at his own home, never wanted to be too far into anyone's life. 'Like I'm going to give someone I hardly know the keys to my apartment.'

'Hardly know?'

'Jack.' She gave up typing and stood, cleared up the noodle boxes and threw them in the bin. 'I'm going to be here till midnight at least—one a.m. at this rate.' She walked over to him, looked down at him and it was as if he made her feel reckless. She couldn't tell him that she adored the distraction, that right now all she wanted was bed and him, but she could not, must not give her heart over to him.

'I really need to work.'

'And I think you deserve a break.' He pulled her onto his lap and they both knew where that had led last time and again he kissed her.

His kiss remained potent and brought her straight back to the places they'd once been. He was unshaven tonight and she felt the scratch on her face and pulled back just a little. 'I need my face for court...'

'Let me kiss you somewhere else, then.'

He was funny and dark and sexy and she had already proved they could work together, that there would be no awkwardness between them whatever went on in the bedroom, but she was not going to love him—all this her eyes told him as she sat there.

'Nina, I know you don't want to hear this, but I want you in a way I have never wanted anyone else...'

'Have me, then.' She wriggled from his lap and he watched her head lower as she bent and removed her boots and her stockings.

'I meant—' Jack's voice was rising '—I want more of you, I want to go out, to do stuff...'

'Jack.' She stood there, bare-legged, bare-bottomed beneath her dress, but she would not bare her heart to him. 'What is it you want? Do you get a kick out of really making someone fall for you, make sure that they're really head over heels and then the second they're yours you dump them?'

Actually, yes, Jack thought, but decided it was better not to voice it.

Because it *was* different this time.

'This is different.' He settled for that.

'Yes, it is,' Nina said. 'You don't have to pretend this is going somewhere—neither of us do.'

'I didn't just come here for sex!'

'Oh, so you didn't bring condoms…' Nina smirked when he didn't reply. 'Not to worry!' She stood over him and kissed him again and his hands held her hips and then slid down to the hem and up her bare legs.

How could this not be enough? Jack reasoned. She matched him sexually and for the first time there was a woman not asking him to change, or where this was leading.

She dropped to her knees then pulled down his scrubs. Her head moved down with the intention to get him out of her office in the space of two minutes and Jack was actually offended. He had never turned down a blow job, had never thought he would, but as he pulled up her head and kissed her, he was, in fact, thoroughly offended.

This was different, his mouth insisted as he wrestled her to the floor.

This was so different, because his mouth was all over her and she was fighting him again. Not the sex, not the attraction, not the passion—she was trying to pretend it was just sex they were having as he was wrestling for her heart.

And she would not give it.

She kissed him back and when he reached into his scrubs for his wallet, again she smirked.

'Told you!'

'Damn it, Nina.' He was getting cross and with women he never did. He just moved happily on when things got too much.

'Shall I help you?'

He pushed her hand off.

He wasn't just angry, he was jealous, but that didn't quite fit, but her sexuality, her detachment, her *oh, a quick orgasm will do, so let's get it over with* was really starting to get to him.

He prised open her legs with his knees and still she kissed him as he stabbed inside her, and she would not give in to him. It was the strangest of fights and as she lay there beneath him he stopped kissing her and lifted onto his elbows and just watched her face. And she decided that she would just give a little bit…

'You're coming out with me.'

'I don't think so.'

'Yeah,' he said, 'you are. I'm taking you away this weekend…' he was moving inside her '…and we're—'

'We can't.'

'We are.'

'I've got Blake.'

God, at every turn she blocked him.

'Sunday night.' Still he moved deep within her.

'I'm busy.'

'I want more of you, Nina.' He was moving too slowly and she wanted him rapid, wanted him near the end, because any more of this and she'd be crying. Any more of this and she'd be sobbing his name and begging for every piece of him.

So she writhed and moaned and said, 'I'm coming…' And she lay there faking it just to finish him.

'Liar.'

He pushed in slower, harder and watched as the tears sprang in her eyes and the colour mounted on her face, as her hips started to lift. 'Please stop.' They both knew she wasn't talking about the sex.

'I want you, Nina.'

'You've got me.'

'I want more of you,' he insisted, and now he moved faster.

And she gave in to her body then, her legs wrapping around him, her arms pulling him in and her mouth claiming his now because if she didn't kiss him hard then she'd tell him she was crazy for him, that she wanted every second of this man. She captured his mouth so he would silence her and then he just exploded. He moved so fast she couldn't breathe and his moan when he came had her shouting his name when she should not have. It was Jack finishing just as she started and he relished every pulse till she faded.

And afterwards he looked down at her, looked right into her eyes, that smile on his face that said *I told you so* and the crush she'd had on him since first they'd met was at dangerous levels now.

Nina didn't really trust anyone and only a fool would trust Jack Carter with their heart and Nina certainly wasn't a fool—she'd seen and experienced far too much of life.

He was dizzy when he climbed off and lay there for a minute. It was Nina who had a very clear head.

She was not going to let him know how she felt about him; she looked over to where he lay with his eyes closed and decided that she'd save that piece for herself, because he was going to hurt her.

She knew it.

In two days or two weeks he would be out of here, and the only way she could carry on working alongside him was if he didn't know he had her heart. There was a very small part of her that pondered, that allowed herself to think, what if? Except it wasn't just about the two of them—Nina came with rather more baggage than most.

'Thank you for a lovely break.' She smiled at him and kissed him. 'And now I really do have to work...'

She really did.

But Nina stopped for a cry a little bit later, because more than anything in the world she wanted her brother and sister, but she'd have also liked a little time to herself, to have said yes to Jack and be going away for a weekend, to just warm herself in the full spotlight of being Jack Carter's lover.

For however long it might last.

CHAPTER NINE

Nina hated going to court.

No, Nina *hated* going to court.

She dressed in her one court outfit and took more care than usual with her hair. Not that it mattered, because it got flattened by her hat as she battled the freezing rain, and when she arrived there and changed from her boots into her shoes, she was reminded again why she hated it so.

There was a ton of work to do back in her office; there were clients she really needed to see, but instead she spent most of the day hanging around court and drinking way too much coffee. When her computer battery died Nina gave up trying to work and read out-of-date magazines, and joy of joys, there was that Christmas one with the Carters on the cover.

She read the article with new eyes now.

Tried not to compare her life to his.

They were lovely people and so was their home.

Anna Carter was a gracious host, she read, who happily showed the reporter around.

Was she jealous as she glimpsed the sumptuous home Jack had grown up in? Or was she just bitter when she read about this close-knit family? How Jack

Senior loved nothing more than a round of golf with his sons and that, yes, Anna couldn't wait until one of her sons gave her grandchildren, which was, she confided, the only thing missing in her very blessed life.

She shouldn't be jealous, Nina reasoned. That wasn't what she was about. She didn't want those sorts of things and, after all, the Carters more than gave back, they were as well known for their charity work as they were for their jet-set lifestyle.

She didn't know how she felt, didn't know why looking at these photos angered her so much. Maybe it was just that she knew she wasn't good enough? Nina had been told that plenty of times in her life, so why would should it be different now?

She felt her phone buzz in her coat, knew it was Jack.

How's court?

Nina didn't answer—after all, she could be in the courtroom now, she reasoned.

How are you?

Nina didn't answer that question either—she simply didn't know.

She'd gone into this thing with him completely aware it was temporary, had shielded herself with that—she just hadn't expected to like him so much. Lust, yes, fancy, yes, but she actually liked him, and maybe she was just fooling herself, maybe it was how Jack played things, but she was actually starting to think that he really liked her, which would be nice and everything, except...

Her phone buzzed again, but it wasn't Jack this time

but Blake, reminding her that she was picking him up at five.

Yes, when she'd far rather be busy, Nina was forced to sit and examine her feelings, because even if Jack might have no intention of ending things any time soon, in just a little while there would be no question of her sleeping over at his place, or long conversations in nice restaurants. There wouldn't even be late nights staying back at the office to catch up on the backlog of work. Instead it would be homework and netball and babysitters...

And as much as she wanted her brother and sister, Nina was honest enough to admit that it was going to hurt to give her freedom up, and that was while knowing how much she loved them.

Why on earth would Jack, who didn't?

The fact-finding hearing finally commenced at two p.m. Nina was actually glad at the effort she had put into the addendum and a judge who listened, because a dispositional hearing was scheduled and Nina breathed a sigh of relief as she stepped out and rang the office with the news.

'Are you coming back in?' Lorianna asked.

'I've got Blake this weekend,' Nina said, 'so it will all just have to wait till Monday.'

'I don't think Jack Carter can wait till then...' Nina rolled her eyes as Lorianna teased, 'He's stopped by here twice, looking for you.'

'To discuss Tommy.' Nina was so not going to fan the gossip. 'He starts his chemotherapy next week and I'm trying to arrange some accommodation nearby for the father.'

She wished Blake's social worker had taken distance into consideration when they had placed Blake. He lived miles from her and, given that she didn't have a car, the trip during peak hour on a Friday night took for ever, as it would when she took him back on Sunday.

She was being ungrateful, Nina thought as she trudged up the Deans' garden path. They were lovely people and had been caring for Blake for the last four years and adored him.

Or had.

When their daughter had emigrated, the Deans had looked into fostering and for three years things had run smoothly. But since their daughter's return from overseas and two new grandchildren to get to know, Blake seemed to be being pushed out more and more. When Nina arrived, Blake was in his room.

'Hi, there, Nina!' Dianne opened the door and invited her in. 'I'll call Blake, he's up in his room.'

Nina stood a little awkwardly in the hallway as Dianne called up to Blake, and though she chatted and was friendly, Nina could hear the laughter and chat coming from the lounge room and knew that Dianne was itching to get back to her family.

'It's my grandson's second birthday.' Dianne smiled. 'We're just having a little party for him.'

'That's lovely.' Nina also smiled.

And it was lovely and completely normal, but she ached for Blake as he came down the stairs. Of course Nina had her doubts at times, of course she questioned taking on so much responsibility, but the second she saw his face any doubts faded.

'Hey, Nina…' He was so pleased to see her and he

asked Dianne if he could show Nina a new poster that he had in his room.

'Why don't you show me when I bring you back?' Nina suggested, because she had that uncomfortable feeling that she and Blake were in the way.

She ached for him.

Ached because for the Wilson siblings love never quite made the distance. Instead, they were always having to make do with someone else's crumbs.

Well, not for much longer.

'Are you looking forward to seeing the new apartment?' Nina asked as they trudged through the slush towards their new home. 'I've got to set up your bed and furniture when we get in. Maybe you can help?'

'I want to watch the game...' Blake was ice-hockey mad, and tonight Nina was actually glad of it as she'd get his room set up much more quickly on her own. 'Can we get take-away?' he asked for maybe the tenth time in as many minutes, refusing to let it drop when Nina said no. And as much as she enjoyed her access times, they were incredibly exhausting too. Nina wanted to be firm with him, but she didn't want to spend the weekend arguing either, and of course she wanted to spoil him. It was conflicting and exhausting and she just wanted Blake properly in her life, not these alternate weekend vacations he expected.

She climbed the stairs to her apartment, Blake still moaning about dinner. She was already peeling off her hat and scarf when she saw Jack standing at her door, holding a bottle of wine.

'What are you doing here?'

'I came to talk to you.'

'I told you I had Blake this weekend.' She looked down at her brother, who was grinning up at Jack, and she was not going to discuss things in front of Blake.

'Go inside, Blake.' She turned the key and pushed open the door. 'I'll be inside in a moment.' And then she remembered that Blake hadn't been there before so she could hardly show him his new home by shoving him inside. Suddenly Nina knew how to sort this right here, right now, knew how to get Jack to leave. 'Come in if you want to…'

She was incredibly annoyed that he did.

Blake raced around the apartment as Jack stood a little awkwardly. 'This is your room,' Nina said. 'I'll make up the furniture later. You go and have a wander around and get used to the place.'

She headed back to Jack.

'I'm sorry,' he said when they were alone. 'I shouldn't have just crashed in like that. I honestly thought when you said weekends that you meant Saturday.'

'Nope,' she said. 'I have Blake two nights a fortnight and soon I'm hoping to make it fourteen.'

She was also incredibly annoyed about what his eyes suggested when she took off her coat and she stood in her court outfit, though it was a little less elegant as she'd changed into boots for the journey home.

'How was court?'

'Good,' Nina said. 'Well, there was a lot of hanging around. I read about you in a magazine, actually…'

'Every word must be true, then.'

'This one was devoid of scandal.' She gave him a smile. 'Your mum can't wait to have grandchildren…'

'Well, she can keep right on waiting.'

She heard the dismissal in his voice and again she was reminded about what she was dealing with.

'Are you close to *anyone*?'

He just gave her a smile that spoke of the other night at the office.

'I'm serious, Jack.'

'As I've said before, there's no such thing as a perfect family.'

'What about your brother?' Nina asked, but Jack shrugged.

'There's a six-year age difference.'

'Same as there is with Janey and Blake,' Nina said. 'There's an even bigger one between Janey and I.'

'Which meant we didn't see each other at school.'

'What about at home?'

'We went to boarding school.' Jack knew his words didn't quite wash, given how she fought so hard to unite her family. 'They're difficult people,' Jack said.

'Families are.'

Blake appeared then, asking again if they could get take-away.

'I've already said no.'

'I don't mind going out to get something...' Jack offered, and had no idea why it incensed her so much, had no idea Blake had been begging for it all the way home.

'I'm *making* dinner,' she said.

'Is that an invitation to join you?''

'It's just pasta.'

'Great.'

Nina slammed around her small kitchen as Jack sat on the sofa, chatting to Blake. She could hear them both laughing and it annoyed her further. 'Jack!' she called over her shoulder as she filled a large saucepan with water. 'Can you come here for a moment?'

'Sure.'

He came to the door.

'Go easy on him.'

'Sorry?'

'Blake's really needy…' She was so angry that he'd turned up like this, because two minutes in it was clear Blake was already a huge Jack Carter fan. 'Just don't make any promises you can't keep.'

'Do you think I'm stupid?'

'No,' Nina answered tartly, 'but we're just friends if he asks.'

'Really!' Jack raised his eyebrows. 'I told Blake I worked with you and had a patient that we needed to discuss, but I can upgrade us to friends if you like…'

'Colleagues is fine.'

Trust Jack to have been one step ahead.

Except she didn't trust Jack, because he was terribly easy to like, and from his past reputation terribly quick to leave.

So she made Blake's favourite dinner, herb and breadcrumb pasta.

Quick, tasty, cheap and *nothing* at all like Jack was used to.

She melted the butter in a pan and added a couple of cups of breadcrumbs and then threw in a load of herbs and tried not to listen to the laughter from the lounge as she put the crumbs into the oven and added the pasta to the water.

He walked into the kitchen and searched for a corkscrew then handed her a glass of wine from the bottle he had brought.

She waited for him to kiss her, to be inappropriate, to cross the line, so she could ask him to leave, but he didn't act inappropriately at all.

'Can I help with anything?'

'Hey, Jack...' Blake called out from the lounge room. 'They're live from The Garden...'

'No TV with dinner,' Nina called.

'Spoilsport.'

Yes, she was a spoilsport, she had to be. She drained the pasta and grated the cheese as Blake set up the table, and she added the herbed breadcrumbs and a load of Parmesan and then took the bowl out to the table.

'Jack goes for the Islanders.' Blake was delighted to have a rival right here in the room and Nina was furious with the schedulers too as she sliced garlic bread. Did tonight have to be the night that Blake's team the New York Rangers clashed with the Islanders?

Of course she would have let Blake watch it. They would have been on the sofa, not at the table, if Jack hadn't arrived.

'Please...' Blake begged.

'Fine,' Nina snapped, and on went the television again and off went the dinner from the table, Blake heaping his bowl and Jack too before heading for the sofa. A reluctant Nina joined them.

'Garlic bread...' She put the steaming plate onto the coffee table.

'Not for me.' Jack smiled. 'I don't want garlic breath.'

Very deliberately she took a piece. And another. She wanted her breath to stink for him and he knew it because he held his fingers in a cross and laughed at her efforts.

It was a brilliant game—possibly the best of the year.

It had sold out weeks ago. Nina knew that because she had been hoping to get tickets and take Blake, but not seeing it live was more than made up for that night.

At times Nina struggled with Blake's needy, demanding ways and she wondered how long it would take Jack to tire of the constant questions, but tonight if anyone was noisy and excessive it was Jack, standing and shouting at the television at times, making Blake laugh at others. She stood in the kitchen, the popcorn popping in the microwave, feeling a lot like the chips she was spitting as a roar went up from the lounge.

'Bite your lip!' Jack shouted as a roar went up from the lounge and she heard Jack explaining illegal hits to Blake in a way Nina never had known how to—that if a player made another bleed, then it meant a longer penalty for the opposing team.

Blake was delighted!

In fact, every word Jack said seemed to have Blake fall in love with him just a little bit more.

'I'm going to set up your room,' Nina said, because she could not stand the adoration on Blake's face. She had honestly thought Jack wouldn't come inside, or if he did that he'd clear off pretty quickly. Now, though, he'd won over another Wilson heart.

'I can do that after the game.' Jack stood in the doorway at the mid-game break and watched her angrily setting up the furniture.

'He'll need to go bed when the game's finished,' Nina said.

'It will take me five minutes.'

'You do a lot of DIY, do you?'

'Fine,' Jack said, 'be a martyr.'

'I'm not being a martyr. I'm just trying to set up his room.'

He didn't get her problem. Jack was having a great evening and just didn't know why it angered her so much, but he gave in then. 'Look, sorry I invaded your time with Blake. I honestly had no idea that he'd be here tonight. My mistake. I can go if you want…'

'You're not *invading* my time with Blake, Jack. I don't think you understand how messed up their lives have been, with people tripping in and out, each one promising that this time things will be different. I don't want that for them here. I don't want my personal life invaded.'

'So you're not going to have friends over or date or…?' He shook his head, went to say something, but Blake called out from the lounge that the game was back on. When Jack headed out, Nina sat back on her heels because, no, she didn't want to make up the bed and, no, she didn't want to be a martyr to her brother and sister, but the last thing she wanted was to hurt them, and losing Jack would hurt.

Perhaps he truly didn't see it.

Didn't fully realise the effect he had on her, the effect he was having on Blake—that if he appeared too long in their lives, it would hurt when he left.

But right now the best she could do was enjoy tonight, so she headed out, sat on the couch next to him and tried to simply live in the here and now, which was actually a very nice place to be, because even when Blake's team lost, he told her he'd still had the best night.

'I'd better go,' Jack said, after he'd finished setting up Blake's room.

'No!' said Blake.

Yes, thought Nina as she walked Jack to the door, but of course Blake didn't want him to leave.

'It's time for you to get ready for bed,' Nina called, but unfortunately she was looking at Jack as she said it.

'It's a bit early for me, but if you insist.'

'Ha-ha.' She stood in her hallway. 'Thanks,' she said. 'Blake had a great night.'

'So did I,' Jack said. 'Don't I get a kiss?'

'I smell of garlic.'

She could hear the phone ringing, wondered who it was this late at night, and the panic that was ever present flared just a touch as Jack carried on, oblivious.

'I love garlic,' he said as he moved in for a kiss.

'Nina…' Blake called. 'They want to speak to you.'

She knew in that moment who it was and walked into the lounge with her heart thumping.

'Nina Wilson.' She closed her eyes, because Jack had followed her back into the lounge and now Jack had a ringside seat to her life. 'No, she hasn't been here.' He watched her open her eyes. 'No, I had no idea. Of course I'll ring…' She took a deep breath. 'If Janey calls, I'll let you know.'

And a lovely, albeit reluctantly lovely, Friday night disappeared in a puff. If she had thought her cheap, herby dinner might put him off and had been wrong, then this surely would.

'Janey's run away.'

'Does she run away a lot?'

Nina shook her head. 'She's been skipping school and there's been just that one time I told you about a few weeks ago when she came to my place...' Nina headed to the window, looked out at the freezing night. She could feel panic squeezing her chest at the thought of Janey out there.

'She's probably gone to a friend's,' Jack reasoned. 'Can you think of anywhere that she might go...?' And then his voice trailed off as the door was pushed open and one very angry young lady walked in.

Jack watched as Nina ran over to her, but Janey pushed her off, anger marring her pretty features as she took in the scene—the scent of dinner still in the air, the popcorn on the coffee table, all evidence of all she had missed out on—then she scowled in Jack's direction. 'Sorry to break up your night. Looks like you've been having fun.'

'Janey...' Nina's voice was strained. 'This is Jack, he's a friend from work. We were...' She shouldn't have to explain herself to Janey, so she didn't. 'Where have you been? Barbara's frantic.'

'I'm not going back.'

'What happened?'

'Barbara wanted me in bed at nine. It's Friday night, for God's sake.'

'Why...?' Nina was trying to stay calm, trying to be reasonable. 'Why did she want you to go to bed at nine?'

Janey shrugged and then sighed out her answer. 'I told you, she's annoyed at me for what happened at netball. I've got to clean the basement.'

'That's not all, though,' Nina broke in. 'I've just been told that she grounded you for skipping school today.'

'Yeah, well, I'm not five—I'm not going to bed at nine. I couldn't even watch the game. Vince came in and told me to turn the television off.'

'Because when you're grounded you're not supposed to be lying in bed, eating popcorn and watching ice hockey.' Nina was struggling not to shout. 'Janey, what do you think it's going to be like when you live with me? There have to be rules…'

'Yeah, well, you just carry on enjoying yourselves,' Janey shouted. 'I'm out of here.'

Jack said nothing, just watched, because trouble hadn't just arrived, Janey was in trouble, a whole lot of it, and he'd dealt with enough to know.

'Why don't you ring them?' Janey challenged. 'And tell them I'm here? Then you can get back to your nice night.'

'You know I have to ring them,' Nina said. 'If I don't they'll soon be here to check after last time. Janey, if I am to have any hope—'

'We'll go to my place.' It was the first words he had spoken since Janey had arrived.

'Jack…' Nina was furious. 'You're just making things worse.'

'Come on.' He ignored her. 'Pack some things.'

'Jack, can I have a word please?'

She had more than a word, she had several heated ones, but Jack stood firm.

'Janey needs to talk to you—she needs some time with you.'

'She doesn't want time with me—every time that I speak to her all she does is walk off,' Nina said.

'Because you get too upset.'

'Of course I get upset! Jack, she came to my office today, moaning about Barbara. She was jealous that Blake was coming here tonight. I knew she was planning trouble...' Nina closed her eyes. 'I have to support Barbara in this. If every time she tries to discipline her, Janey comes running to me, things aren't going to get any better. I'll speak with Barbara and suggest that if Janey gets the basement sorted then she can come and spend Sunday night with me.'

'She won't and you know it,' Jack said. 'If you send her back now, or they put her in a temporary placement, she's just going to be a whole lot angrier at you. Now, let's go to my apartment and from there we can sort things, but any minute now you'll have the department knocking, especially if they found her here last time.'

He was right, so Nina grabbed a few things and a few minutes later her little family was sitting in Jack's car, Blake beside himself he was so delighted, Janey angry and silent. Nina just quietly panicked, embarrassed by the chaos of her life and unsure this was the right thing to do.

'We need to ring them.'

'And we will. We're not fugitives.' He turned and smiled at her. 'You've got access to Blake, Janey's nearly sixteen, you're her sister...'

'Could this get you into trouble?'

'No.' He shook his head. 'I'm doing what I think is right and I'll tell that to anyone who asks. I am not having her taken back just to run away again.' He glanced in the rear-view mirror and met the hostile stare of Janey. 'We'll be there soon.'

As expected, she didn't reply.

His apartment was huge, but not designed for children. Blake was at his most annoying, running around, while Janey just sat silently on one of his lovely white sofas. All Nina could think was that they were all so out of place in his perfect life.

Even Jack was wondering what on earth to do with them. Yes, there were spare bedrooms but somehow a luxurious bachelor pad wasn't really conducive to talking, not with a messed-up teenager anyway.

He didn't do the family thing, had never had the family thing himself. The only time he'd done anything remotely family-like had been… And it was then that Jack had an idea and he turned to Janey.

'You're to ring Barbara and tell her that you're safe, that you're with your sister, and that you're going away for the weekend.'

'Jack!'

He turned to an angry Nina. 'And you're to ring back Janey's worker and tell her the same,' he said to Nina's rigid face. 'She's not in any danger, she's with her sister who has access, so just tell them that you'll bring Janey in on Monday morning to the office.'

'So they can send me back.' Janey looked at him.

'I don't know,' he admitted. 'But running away isn't helping things.'

Janey just turned her head away and carried on staring out of the window and then did the same in the car as they left Manhattan.

Of course he'd have a place in the Hamptons, Nina thought darkly as the car drove through the night.

They stopped for provisions and she was glad that he didn't embarrass her by offering money, just suggested she get a few warm things. She bought some food too as Blake raced around the aisles of the store and Janey just walked silently beside her. As they stepped out into the parking lot she half expected Jack to be gone, but of course he wouldn't do that, Nina knew. He'd probably drop them off at his mansion and then belt it back to Manhattan.

Still, she was grateful to him.

His stern words had helped her handle the department and this small window of time with Janey might mean that hopefully, hopefully she could get to the bottom of things.

'Wow!' Blake was wide awake and admiring the huge houses they passed. 'Is this yours?' he asked as they slowed down.

'Nope.'

'This one?'

'Nope.'

And then Jack indicated, they turned into a small street and Jack parked.

'We'll have to walk from here.'

It was a tiny house on a large block and they couldn't park in the drive because it was covered in thick snow.

It was actually funny trying to get to the door. Jack put Blake on his back and even Janey laughed as, up to their knees, they waded through snow and he deposited them inside and then went back to the car and got all their bags.

They were all soaked and the house was colder inside than out.

They walked into the lounge and Jack lit a fire that had been prepared and reminded himself to leave a big tip for the cleaning lady who came in and aired the place regularly. They all stood shivering as the fire took. 'There are a couple of heaters I can set up in your rooms…' He looked at Blake and Janey. 'I'll go and check things out. Janey, can you make something to drink?'

Nina followed him, dragging the heaters into the small bedrooms, and she looked around. 'I was expecting a mansion.'

'Disappointed?'

'No, it's lovely, just cold.'

'Yeah, well, not for long. I'm just waiting for planning permission then the bulldozers will be in.'

Once the heaters were on in the kids' rooms he showed her the main bedroom.

'You'll freeze,' Jack said.

'I'll be fine.'

They went back through to the living area and Janey had actually done as she'd been asked and made everyone a drink. By the time they'd finished, it was terribly late and Blake was falling asleep on the sofa. When Nina returned from taking him to his bed, Janey was already heading off to hers.

'Janey, wait,' Nina called, but Janey wasn't hanging around to talk to her.

''Night.'

They sat in the lounge and when finally they were alone, Jack closed the door and spoke to her.

'Are you sure you want to do this?' Jack said, and she sat there silent as he spoke on. 'Are you absolutely sure that you want full custody?'

She looked at Jack and she knew it was their death knell, knew that it would be the end of them, and even though it hurt like hell, yes, she was sure and she nodded.

'Because if I go into bat for you...' Jack looked at her '...you'll get it. I always win.'

'Not always,' she said. 'You didn't win with Sienna.'

'That's because I privately thought you were right,' Jack said. 'If I hadn't there would have been no way Sienna would have gone home to the care of her mother. I just want to be completely sure that this is what you want.'

'Yes,' Nina said. 'I want my family together.'

'Then we'll sort it out, but right now you need to back off from Janey and stop trying to get her to talk to you.'

'I need to know what's going on.'

'She'll tell you when she's ready. Right...' Jack stood. 'I'm going to drive back.' They headed out to the hall. 'Will you be all right without a car?'

'I don't have a car anyway.' Nina smiled. 'I'm sure I can work out how to call for a taxi.'

'I'm sure you can.' He gave her a kiss, but not a long one as it really was terribly late now. 'I'll pick you up on Sunday afternoon.'

'We're taking up all your weekend,' Nina apologised, her hands loosely together behind his neck.

Jack wasn't quite so tired now. 'You could take up a bit more.'

He watched the smile at the edges of her mouth.

'I don't want you freezing...' Jack moved to her ear.

'It is terribly cold,' Nina admitted.

'Then it's the least I can do.' Jack smiled.

They had never undressed more quickly, though Nina kept her underwear and T-shirt on to take off once they were in bed and they dived under the covers. Jack turned to her.

'You smell of garlic.'

'It was supposed to be a deterrent.'

'Not for me.'

She wriggled away, but he pulled her back. 'We have to keep warm.' He pulled at her T-shirt. 'Skin on skin,' Jack said, and he peeled off all her clothing. 'That's how you prevent hypothermia. I did mountain rescue once.'

She laughed.

'I didn't really,' he admitted.

But it was exactly how it felt.

As if they were happily trapped on a ledge, waiting, while not wanting the cavalry to arrive, freezing cold and staying warm by the favourite method of all. Afterwards she thanked him for his help with her family and for how he'd handled things tonight.

'I know I try too hard with them,' Nina said. 'You know what it's like with family...' Then she remembered their earlier conversation. 'I thought you all got on?'

'That's what they want people to think,' Jack said. 'We're hardly going to air everything in public but, no, I really couldn't care less about them.'

And he said it so easily, was just so matter-of-fact as he dismissed his entire family, and just a few moments later Nina realised he was asleep. She lay there half the night thinking about the wonderful family he cared so little about and fully realised the impossibility of him ever really caring for hers.

CHAPTER TEN

'Do you come here a lot?' They lay in bed in the morning, before the day had started, and she looked at the man who had brought her family here, who had given them a chance to get away from things properly.

He turned and gave her that devilish smile. 'It depends what this morning brings.' And she simply smiled, except Jack did not. He didn't really want to talk about his time here, but realising all she had trusted him with last night, maybe it was fair to be a bit more open than he would be usually.

'I came on holiday here when I was younger, stayed in a house close to here.' He didn't actually tell her it was the same house.

'Do your family have a property here too, then?'

'They have a property nearby but, no, I came here with a school friend and I stayed with his family.'

'Good?' Nina asked.

'It was great,' Jack said. 'Best summer of my life. We didn't do much really—just the beach most days. I bought this place last year when it came on the market and I thought it was too good to pass up. I'm getting plans drawn up. I want to build up and get the view...'

'And get heating.'

'Oh, yes.' They lay in silence for a moment and then Jack turned and looked at her very serious face, could almost hear her worrying about what to say to Janey, how to approach things with her sister. 'You need to relax.'

'I know.'

'You get too tense.'

'Thanks, Jack,' she snapped, but she knew he was right. 'I don't know what to do today—I mean, she's hardly going to want to build a snowman.'

'There's loads to do here.'

'Like what?'

'Outdoor ice skating,' Jack said, 'and there's a whale tour, it's supposed to be fantastic.'

'How do you know?'

Jack would rather face the freezing morning than deal with that topic. He'd already said far too much, way more than he usually would, and so he pulled back the blankets and climbed out. 'I'm going to get the fire in the lounge going and then sort out breakfast.' He shook his head as she went to climb out. 'Stay there,' he offered. 'I'll bring you in a coffee.'

Jack set to work building the fire and then he headed off to make coffee, and as he returned with two mugs, he nodded to Janey, who was huddled on the couch. 'Still here? I thought you'd be out the window.'

Janey gave a reluctant half-smile. 'Yeah, well, I didn't fancy freezing to death.'

'Did you want a coffee?' Jack asked. 'I just made some.'

Another shrug and then a nod and when she told him she took it the same as Nina he handed her Nina's mug and then went and made a fresh one, then headed back into the bedroom.

'Janey's up, but not Blake.'

'She's up…' Nina went to pull back the blankets, but Jack very deliberately sat down on her side of the bed.

'Leave her.'

'But it might be a good chance to talk to her, before Blake gets up.'

'Which is why she's probably sitting on that couch waiting for the door to open,' Jack said. 'She was waiting for a lecture from me or an, oh, so casual talk from you. Just let her relax…'

'It's so hard, though.'

'Which is why it's good you've got the whole weekend. Look, I'll head back soon and you guys can just have some time—she'll talk when she wants to, Nina.'

'And if she doesn't?'

'Then she was never going to.'

He'd been working with children a long time and was actually very good with adolescents, his slightly aloof, completely unshockable stance giving them confidence. More than most, Jack understood that things weren't always as they seemed—was never blindsided by the persuasive words of the parents.

They drank their coffee and then headed out, only to be met by the delicious smell of breakfast coming from the kitchen. Nina realised that had she got out of bed the minute Jack had told her that Janey was up, had she dashed to the living room for the essential talk, then this might never have happened. Blake and Janey, standing in the kitchen and serving up a delicious breakfast of pancakes and sausages and eggs from the ingedients that Nina had bought from the store last night.

'This looks lovely.'

'I'm starving,' Jack said, and watching Janey serve up he reminded her that Nina was a vegetarian. 'No sausages for your sister.'

'It's...' She felt Jack's hand squeeze hers, realised she must not make too much of a fuss. 'I'll set the table.'

Jack helped, and not just with the cutlery.

'Janey is nearly sixteen,' he pointed out. 'She should be making breakfast, Nina.'

'And she is.'

'And you should be allowed to say you're a vegetarian and that you don't eat sausages.' He looked at her. 'You would have eaten them, wouldn't you?'

'Of course not.'

'Liar.' Jack grinned. 'You'd go against every one of your principles just to please her. You don't have to be her mum.'

'I know that. But she needs more than just a big sister.'

'No,' Jack said. 'She just needs you to be you and she needs to take on some of the responsibility too. What were you doing at that age?'

He left her for a moment to ponder and when he returned with orange juice and glasses she answered his question, because at fifteen years old her part-time job in the hardware store had made a vital contribution to the family.

'Working,' Nina said. 'And going to school. We weren't exactly well off.' And though he appeared unmoved, Jack was far from it, especially when, as they sat eating breakfast, talking and laughing, Janey had mentioned their mum and the Mother's Day breakfast they'd shared just before she'd died.

'Nina did all the cooking then,' Janey said. 'I just got to pour on the maple syrup.' And he felt his stomach tighten as he realised, perhaps properly, all she had been through. That Nina hadn't been much older than Janey was now when she had lost her parents, and the thought of her so young and alone and dealing with such grief brought out a rare surge of compassion in him.

Not that he showed it.

Instead, because they'd cooked, he found out that meant he and Nina were doing the dishes and he grumbled all the way through it. Then Janey grumbled when Nina suggested they go on the whale boat trip.

'You're going,' Jack said in the end to Janey. 'You can miserable with me.'

And though Nina wanted him gone, there was a sigh of relief she held onto because handling the two of them was just so much easier when he was around. Maybe because he was actually old enough to be their parent— the nine years Jack had on her made a big difference.

'Thanks,' Nina said again.

'No need to thank me.'

They were impossible to get out of the house, Jack realised.

Janey took for ever in the bathroom and came out fully made up, while Blake had zero attention span and had to be told five times to wash and get dressed. Nina thought that Jack, with his streamlined life, would get irritated, because it was close to eleven by the time they all headed off, but he didn't seem fazed at all.

Jack talked to Blake in the car about the hockey game the previous night and Janey moaned that the last thing she wanted to see was a group of whales.

'A pod of whales.' Jack turned briefly from the driving seat. 'It's a pod of whales, not a group of whales.'

Nina rolled her eyes, surprised when Janey giggled.

On deck, it was absolutely freezing, but the cabin was warm and there was endless hot chocolate. They took it in turns to go in and out, but it was more than worth it when finally a *pod* of whales was spotted. Far from being bored by them, Janey and Blake stayed on deck for ages—it was Nina and Jack who ducked in for some warmth.

'Thanks for this,' Nina said. 'They've had the best day.'

'What about you?' Jack asked.

'It's been brilliant,' Nina said. 'I really do appreciate it.' She didn't dare ask Jack what sort of day he was having—he'd been so kind to take them on, but surely this wasn't his ideal way to spend a weekend. After all, he had admitted that he rarely used the house and playing carer to two rather troubled foster-children on a rare weekend off no doubt had him wondering why on earth he had got involved with her.

He was very quiet on the drive home.

He told Nina about a couple of local restaurants, but apart from that he didn't say much.

'I'm tired,' Blake said.

'Can we just stay home and eat?' Janey asked.

They'd spent one night there and already Janey had referred to it as home.

It was how he had felt many years ago.

Yes, Jack was quiet.

They arrived back at the house and Jack saw them in.

'Where are you going?' Blake asked when after a quick drink Jack said goodbye.

'Jack's going home.' Nina smiled. 'It's Saturday night!' she said as she followed him out to the hall

'Thanks again.' Nina smiled.

He kissed her more thoroughly than he had the last time they had been in this hall, wondered perhaps if he could be persuaded to stay again.

'Have a great night…' It was Nina who pulled back.

'Sure,' Jack said. 'You too.' He was just a tiny bit rattled and couldn't work out why. 'What do you think you'll do?'

'I'm sure we'll find something, and we might try ice skating tomorrow…' She gave him another kiss. 'See you then.'

'Nina…' He should really just turn and go, really not say what he was about to, but his mouth was moving faster than his brain. 'What was that little snipe for?'

'When?'

'"It's Saturday night!"'

'Well, it *is* Saturday night and I remember you telling me you hadn't had one off in ages that hadn't been taken up by social and networking events,' Nina said. 'It wasn't a snipe.'

'You're sure?' Jack checked.

'Jack…' Nina was not going to get into this. 'I hope you have a good night.'

And he drove off towards the lights of a very busy city. Jack knew how to spend a free Saturday night. And he was free, he told himself when he headed to his favourite bar and met up with a few colleagues. But when he found himself being chatted up by an exceptionally good-looking brunette, whose baggage contained only the lipstick it held, he couldn't seem to concentrate on the conversation. His mind kept drifting back to the house and all that was going on there.

And he was free too to leave the bar alone, even to the pout of the stunning brunette, but Jack was unsettled and even a bit angry.

Nina hadn't even asked him about his plans.

Which was how he wanted things. The last thing he wanted was to get involved in a *relationship* with Nina Wilson, and the irony that he had revised that from *fling* wasn't lost on Jack.

She was carer to two children and he wanted none of that.

He wanted straightforward, uncomplicated, and Nina was none of that either.

'Jack!' As the lift door opened he saw Monica standing there, not in tears this time but wearing a smile.

'What are you doing here?'

'As you said, there doesn't always have to be a reason…'

Jack smiled as she walked over to him, but it sort of halted on his lips as he said words he'd thought he never would.

'I'm seeing someone.'

He was, and for the first time he said it.

'What?' Monica smiled. 'For all of two weeks? It can't be that serious.' She pressed her lips to him, ran her hands down his chest.

'Yeah, well, it is.' Jack's hands halted hers.

'Doesn't matter...' Monica purred.

But as he kissed her back, Jack knew that it did, that for the first time he was serious about a woman and that he could be about to lose his formidable 'between the sheets' reputation here, because he wasn't even turned on. He stopped kissing her back, because he wasn't enjoying it and because...

'Actually, it does matter.'

He saw Monica to the lift and then let himself in and checked his phone. No, of course Nina hadn't called him.

Neither did he call her, because for the first time he was seeing someone, for the first time things were starting to look serious, for Jack at least.

He had no idea how Nina felt. She seemed delighted to keep things casual, didn't care a bit that he was out tonight.

Jack didn't know what to think.

CHAPTER ELEVEN

'JACK!'

Blake was delighted to see him. 'Janey got hurt.'

'I'm fine,' Janey insisted. 'I fell over, ice skating.' She rolled up her sleeve and showed a rather spectacular bruise, as Nina came through to the lounge and he saw the tension on her face.

'Great, isn't it?' She rolled her eyes. 'I'm sending her back black and blue.'

'It was an accident, ice skating,' Jack calmly pointed out.

'It will be fine, Nina,' Janey said, and he heard the younger sister trying to reassure the older, actually heard the rare tenderness in Janey's voice. And despite appearances, despite the horrible things she said at times, Jack realised Janey really did love Nina.

'So how did you all go?' Jack followed her into the bedroom where Nina was packing.

'Okay, I guess, but Janey took herself off to bed at eight last night and this morning she didn't want to talk. Still, it was fun ice skating till she fell. How was your night?'

'Yeah, okay.' He didn't even have to be evasive, Nina simply didn't want the details.

Everyone was trying to ignore that the small holiday was over, trying to pretend that everything was fine. It was Blake who couldn't hold out.

'I don't want to go back.'

Jack was loading up the car when Blake said it.

'I know,' Nina answered, as she always did, because Blake never wanted to go back, only this time it was different. 'Couldn't we stay another night?' Janey asked.

'We can't,' Nina replied. 'Blake's got school tomorrow and we've got to go and sort things out.'

Nina watched as Jack locked up the house and when he climbed into the car and drove off, he didn't really say much. For once it was Janey who was talking.

'What are we doing tonight?'

'Sleeping,' Nina said. 'And we can set up your bedroom.'

'Jack can do that,' Janey said.

'Uh-oh…' Jack shook his head. 'I've got to head home once I've dropped you guys off.' He glanced in the mirror as he said it and saw Janey's frown, but didn't pay too much attention to it.

'I think I might go back to Barbara's tonight.' Janey's voice from the back seat broke into her thoughts.

'Barbara's?' Nina swung around. 'I thought the whole point of running away was because you didn't want to ever go back there!'

'Yeah, well, I've changed my mind.'

'Janey…' Nina was struggling to keep exasperation out of her voice. 'Let's just leave things as they are. We can have a nice night, just the two of us, and sort things out, talk things out…'

Jack glanced in the mirror again and saw that Janey was back to looking out of the window, realising then that the last thing Janey wanted was another night alone with Nina.

Why?

He said nothing, just kept driving, but his mind was working overtime.

Why wouldn't Janey want a night alone with her big sister? He went through things just as he would with a patient, doing his best to take all the emotion out—except it was impossible to extract emotion from this equation.

Janey was back to scowling and as they approached Manhattan Blake started to cry.

'I'll see you in a couple of weeks.' Nina daren't say it might be sooner, not until she had spoken with his social worker. There was an appointment next week for them to come and see her flat—the wheels tended to move really slowly when a child wasn't in danger. Jack said nothing. He really didn't know how to deal with the situation. He could see Janey's angry expression in the rear-view mirror, could almost feel the daggers she was hurling at him embedding in his back.

'Just here,' Nina said as they approached the house where Blake lived, and Jack wondered how she did this every fortnight. Saying goodbye once was bad enough, but having to do it week in and week out must kill her. He helped her to get Blake's case out of the boot and saw her pale face as she did her best to stay calm for Blake, who was really crying now and clinging to her.

'Of course you can show me your poster.' She glanced up at Jack. 'I might be a while.'

'Take your time.'

'Can Jack come and see it?' Blake asked hopefully, but Jack shook his head.

'I'm going to wait in the car.'

Nina didn't blame him. He wasn't trying to impress Blake, or be his best friend, or proxy father, but she felt the sting of his rejection and it compounded her thoughts that she must end this soon, because after just one weekend Blake already hero-worshipped him. He'd already had enough loss in his life and she didn't want him falling in love with Jack, only to lose him too.

In fact, Jack would've loved to have made this transition easier for Blake, would have happily gone in and looked at his hockey posters, but he had a feeling that there was a rather more difficult conversation to be had and that it was about to take place.

Jack's instincts were rarely wrong.

'Happy now?' Janey demanded as soon as he got into the car. 'You give him the best weekend, driving around in your flash Jag, and then drop him back...' She was going ballistic and Jack just sat there. 'Mr Nice Guy!' Janey sneered, and Jack sat there as she told him how he thought he was better than them, better looking than them and that he was messing around with her sister.

Jack anticipated what would come next, warned Janey that if she spoke like that again, he would get out of the car and go and get Nina, which was when Janey burst into tears. In the end there was no need for a long talk—all Jack really had to do was listen.

'Can you tell Nina this?' Jack asked.

'No,' Janey sobbed. 'Because she panics about everything, she feels guilty about everything. I know you think she's good at her job, and calm about things, but she loses her temper when it comes to us and she'll go crazy when she finds out...'

And Jack smiled an invisible smile, because Nina would do that. 'I'm scared she'll get into trouble and lose her job or something.'

'Your sister is not going to get into trouble,' Jack assured her, 'and neither are you—you've done nothing wrong.' He was very certain on that. 'Can I speak with Nina about it?' he asked. 'I can come back to the apartment and we can talk about it tonight...'

'No!' Janey begged, her hand moving to open the door.

'Don't run off, Janey.' Jack was stern and she shrank back in the seat. He would have spoken some more but all too soon Nina was coming out of the house, doing her best not to cry, waving to a tearful Blake, and somehow Jack had to sort this, would sort this, but he wondered how best to go about it. Nina was going to freak, he knew that, which meant Janey was likely to run again...

'Please don't say anything,' Janey begged as Nina got into the car, all falsely bright and cheerful.

'Right.' She smiled at Janey. 'Let's get back to the flat.'

Except there was no way Jack was going to drop the two of them off at Nina's flat.

'We could go back to my place,' he suggested.

'No.' Nina was adamant. 'I want to have some time with Janey before we go to the social worker in the morning.'

Jack drove through the wet streets, his mind working overtime, but as they drove past Central Park he knew what to do and Jack indicated and turned into the hospital.

'Do you need to check on someone?' Nina asked as Jack slid into his reserved parking spot.

'No,' Jack said. 'I want to get Janey's elbow examined.'

'It's just a bruise,' Nina said. 'I know I made a fuss, but I was just worried about having to face the social worker tomorrow with Janey covered in bruises. I was being ridiculous. She's fifteen, she fell, ice skating…'

'Still, it's better to get it all documented,' Jack said, getting out of the car and holding the door open for Janey.

Nina frowned, surprised that Jack thought it necessary, but more surprised that Janey so willingly got out of the car.

They walked into Emergency and Jack had a word with one of the nurses to ask which doctors were on.

'She doesn't need to see the Head of Emergency,' Nina said, when she heard Jack asking for Lewis to examine Janey.

'He's a great guy,' Jack said. 'I trust him implicitly.' He gave Janey a thin smile. 'I'll just go and have a word with him. Nina, why don't you get Janey into a gown? He'll need to examine her for range of movement…'

He wanted Lewis to see Janey, and with good reason. Not only was Lewis an excellent doctor and trusted colleague, but he would understand more than most the complexities of dealing with a very troubled young girl.

'I'd rather you hear it from Janey.' Jack spoke briefly with Lewis. 'Assuming, that is, that she talks, but basically we're not here about her elbow.'

'Right.' Lewis nodded.

'And if she doesn't talk to you,' Jack said, 'then maybe she might need a night of observation waiting for the orthos to have a look.'

'Let's just see how it goes,' Lewis suggested. 'She's here with her sister?'

'Nina Wilson, the social worker.' Jack nodded. 'She thinks that I've brought Janey here just to get her arm examined, but whatever happens I'm going to have to step in. I'm just hoping that Janey will talk to you.'

'Sure.' Lewis nodded. 'How about you introduce me?' Lewis called for one of the senior nurses to go in with him and smiled and introduced himself to an anxious-looking Janey.

'Okay,' Jack said. 'Nina and I are going to go and get a coffee. As I said, Lewis is a friend of mine, you're in very good hands.'

It was only then that it dawned on Nina what was happening, or maybe it had started to a couple of moments before. She was about to say no, to insist she was staying with Janey, but she realised then that there was another reason that Jack had brought them here. She had seen scenarios like this on endless occasions. She was being removed from Janey to give her sister a chance to talk.

'Sure!' Nina choked back the sudden tears that were threatening. 'I could use a coffee.'

Nina waited till they were well away from the cubicle before she spoke. 'Jack, what's going on?'

'Just come in here and have a seat, Nina.'

'You think I did it.'

'Nina.' He shook his head. 'Not for a second did it enter my head that you'd hurt your sister.' Then he was honest. 'I did wonder why she didn't want to spend a night with you, but I think we both know that I don't jump to conclusions.'

He didn't know whether to tell her just yet, but at that moment a nurse popped her head out. 'Jack, Janey wants you to be in there when she speaks to Lewis.'

Nina stood.

'She wants me,' Jack said.

'Why not me?' Nina demanded. 'Why can't she speak to me?'

'Because she's been trying to spare your feelings,' Jack said. 'Because she doesn't love me and she knows I'm not going to get upset or angry or do anything rash, so just have a seat, Nina, and I'll be back to you as soon as I can.'

'Have you any idea how hard this is?' she demanded. 'You gave me no clue. All weekend you never gave a hint you were going to do this.'

'I didn't know then,' Jack said, and he was just so matter-of-fact and calm about everything. 'Nina, she said something in the car that I can't ignore but, please, you just have to trust that I am doing the very best I can for both you and Janey, and right now that means that I've got to go.'

It killed Nina to sit there not knowing what was going on. What on earth had Janey said in the car? Had she threatened to self-harm or was she doing drugs? She'd certainly been withdrawn at times. Or maybe she was pregnant? Nina sat there for what felt like an eternity before Jack finally returned, his face grim. He gave her a thin smile and then took a seat next to her.

'She's fine.'

Nina blew out her breath. 'But?'

Jack looked at her tense face and the bundle of passion that was Nina and didn't blame Janey a bit for not wanting to be the one to tell her.

'Barbara, her foster-mother, has got a new boy-friend, Vince…'

'Oh, God!' Nina stood. She just wanted to dash out there, to be with Janey, but again Jack was stern.

'Sit down, Nina, you need to hear this. First of all, nothing has happened, well, not what you're dreading, at least I don't think so, but you need to listen and then calm down and *then* you can go in and speak to Janey.'

'So he hasn't touched her?'

'He's tried to.'

Jack was very calm and annoyingly matter-of-fact, but sadly he dealt with this type of problem all too often, and though it was upsetting a cool head was needed. Jack was very good at that, except as he went through it with Nina he felt his anger starting to rise, an anger that he had to work hard to keep in check. The detachment that made this job easier for Jack was dissipating by the moment as he told Nina all that had happened.

'When you took Blake inside, she got very angry with me, told me I didn't care, that I'd made things harder for Blake, all that sort of thing.' Nina nodded, because that sounded very like Janey. 'Then she said I was up myself with my flash car and my good looks…'

Nina frowned. 'Then she made a couple of suggestions and I told her that if she carried on like that I would get out of the car and go and get you.'

'Suggestions?'

'She was testing me, Nina, being deliberately provocative, and when I was having no part of it she broke down and started to cry. You know teenage girls do that sometimes, and most guys in an authoritative position know how to deal with that.'

Nina started to cry, because of all the things she'd dreaded hearing, this was the one she'd dreaded the most.

'Vince has been coming in to say goodnight to her.' Nina started to retch and he handed her the bin as she struggled to take breaths. She heard stuff like this every day, but it killed her to think it had happened to Janey. 'She didn't like it and she told Barbara, but then she got told off, because Barbara said it was nice that her boyfriend was making an effort. He's been creeping Janey out and she felt that she had to start getting dressed in the bathroom, because he was always finding an excuse to come into her room. Even when she was sent to bed early, or late, or whatever, he'd come in. He's tried a couple of times to kiss her, made a few inappropriate comments, and basically she's been fending him off.'

'I'll kill him.' Nina could hardly breathe. She wanted to go there right now, right this minute, and she told Jack exactly what she'd do when she got there. Jack just sat there as she ranted on for a while till she got back to Janey. 'Why couldn't she tell me?'

'Because she didn't want to watch you retching into

a bin, because she knew you'd get upset and feel guilty, that you'd think it was your fault...'

'It is, though,' Nina sobbed. 'It's my job to pro-tect—'

'Nina!' Jack was firm. 'You are not allowed to have your sister as a client for a very good reason. Right now the hospital social worker is coming down to see her, and it will all be dealt with properly. The main thing is, she is not going back there.'

'Can I speak to her?'

'In a moment, when you've calmed down.'

It actually took more than a moment for Nina to calm down. She couldn't stop crying and Lewis came in and had a word with her and confirmed all that Jack had said. 'She's fine, just relieved that she's told some-one. In fact, she's more worried about you.'

'I've calmed down now,' Nina said, and she looked at Jack. 'I'm actually glad that she told you. I'd have reacted terribly. It's just impossible to think of it as an-other job. It's different when it's your family.'

'Of course it is,' Jack said. 'You should go and see her.'

Nina nodded.

She was determined to be calm when she walked in there, but she burst into tears when she cuddled Janey, and Janey burst into tears too. After a few min-utes they calmed down and a while later, Jack popped his head in.

'How are things?'

'Better,' Janey said, and then her eyes filled up with fresh tears. 'I'm sorry for all the things I said.'

'Yeah, well, you had a good reason,' Jack said. 'But what's wrong with my car?'

Janey even managed her first laugh since her arrival at Angel's. 'How was she when you told her?' Janey nodded in the direction of Nina.

'Pretty much as you'd expect!'

'I am here,' Nina said. 'I took it quite well.'

'Oh, God!' Jack impersonated her, and Janey smiled. 'I handed her the bin…'

'I wasn't that bad.'

'You were fine.' Jack smiled.

'Thank you,' Nina said. He really had been marvellous. 'We're going to be here ages, so you might as well go home. Thank you so much for everything.'

'I'll stick around for a while.'

'You really don't have to.'

'It's fine.'

It was a very long night. Things like this were dealt with thoroughly and given that Barbara had two other foster-children, Child Protection went around to speak with the family, but Vince was out and Barbara angrily denied there had been anything inappropriate taking place, Nina was informed by her friend and colleague. 'She's very angry with Janey,' Lorianna told her. 'The usual stuff, but don't worry…'

'I want my sister and my brother in my care.'

'It sounds as if Blake is doing fine.'

'No!' Nina said. 'Blake is not fine, Blake *is* being looked after but he's not being loved. He's clingy and needy and he needs to be with his family.'

Jack listened to her fighting for her brother and sister, saw the determination in Nina's eyes and that she would not back off, would not wait for the department to take its time. This was going to be dealt with, and soon, she told Lorianna.

Jack went and got a drink from the water cooler and just stood and looked around the familiar department, except everything felt unfamiliar. He was glad to be there, glad to have helped, and despite Nina insisting that he go home, Jack actually didn't want to, he really wanted to be here and see things through.

'I thought you were off.' Alex caught up with him at the water cooler. 'How come you're here?'

'Personal stuff,' Jack said, but it was more than personal, it actually felt like family—better than family, in fact.

No one tried to spare anyone's feelings in his family. There were, Jack had long since concluded, no feelings to spare.

Imagine Nina when she met his family—she'd run a mile, Jack knew it. Still, he wasn't going to talk about that with Alex. Instead, he asked about another young patient who, thanks to a certain young woman, had been on his mind of late.

'How's Tommy doing?'

'He's had a good weekend,' Alex said. 'They're starting the treatment tomorrow and hopefully there will be a good response. We should be able to buy him some time.'

'Surgery?'

Alex grimaced. 'I think time is all we can hope for.'

'But do you think it could be an option…' Jack knew he was pushing things, knew what Alex's problem was, but Alex wasn't in the mood to open up either. 'You've done similar surgery before.'

'Thanks for that, Jack,' Alex snapped, but still Jack wouldn't back off.

'If you want to talk…'

'Again—thanks.'

'I mean it, Alex.'

But Alex stalked off. Jack had clearly got to him, but just as he was pondering how better to discuss things, Jack was distracted by an irate man storming through the department. 'Where is she?' Security was pulling him back, keeping him well away from the patients, and Jack walked over to the waiting room where the man was still ranting. Unable to calm him down, Security took him outside.

'She's a lying bitch,' he shouted, and Jack looked at him, felt the anger he'd never felt before slowly building. 'Janey's a liar, I never laid a finger on her…'

And while Jack should have been thinking about his career, the newspapers, the hospital, his role, none of that entered his head. Instead, he just stared at the piece of filth that had tried to touch Nina's little sister and as detached and dispassionate as he could be at times, tonight just wasn't one of those times.

'It was her that came on to me,' Vince shouted, 'flaunting her…' He didn't get to finish.

Jack's fist met his jaw, and two rather startled security guards had to let Vince go. After all, they could hardly hold him as the Head of Paediatrics hit him.

And that was what greeted Nina's eyes when she walked outside.

Vince sprang and lunged at Jack, who met him with

his fist again, and Nina stood there just a little bit torn, because she abhorred violence, there really was no place for it in Nina's book, but seeing Jack's fist mid swing and one blackening eye, seeing someone for the first time truly fighting for her family, seeing Jack doing to Vince what she could have so easily done herself, she was hard placed not to stand there cheering.

Still, the fight was broken up quickly and when Vince shouted he that was going to press charges, Nina saw a very different Jack from the one she thought she knew. He was being held back by Security, telling Vince to go ahead, that he was looking forward to seeing him in court where he could explain himself...

Of course there was no chance of keeping things quiet.

Not a hope. It was all around the hospital by the time Jack's closing eye was being treated with an ice pack and even though Nina had tried to keep it from Janey, of course gossip was rife in the corridors and she'd heard people talking.

'Did he hit him?' Janey was sitting on a hospital trolley and was absolutely delighted. 'Did Jack really hit him? That's brilliant!'

'It is so not brilliant,' Nina scolded. 'There's no excuse for violence.'

And there would be ramifications for it too, Nina fretted when she had a word with Lewis a little later. 'Do you think he'll get into trouble?'

'Who, Jack?' Lewis shook his head. 'Not a chance. Really, it's the other guy who needs to be worried. I tell you, I cheered inside. Sometimes in this job you'd love to forget the law...'

'I know,' Nina said. 'Except we don't!' She really couldn't get her head around it, but Lewis was talking about Janey now.

'I've spoken to Social Services and given you already have reprieve access with her, we could send Janey home with you tonight, but I've spoken at length with Lorianna and we both agree that if we do a case meeting in the morning, once they've spoken with Blake's case worker, it might just push things along. It's not the hospital department we're dealing with, but we might stand more of a chance of moving things along than you'll have once Janey is home.'

'I know.'

'So let's keep Janey here and we'll roll the ball a bit harder tomorrow morning.'

He'd been marvellous and again Nina thanked him, before going in to say goodnight to Janey. Jack stood with his keys, trying not to yawn as she said goodbye.

'Jack's going to give me a lift home. We both need to get some rest. It's going to be a busy day tomorrow,' Nina said, and she saw the worry return to Janey's face. 'And I am going to do everything I can to make sure that you and Blake are home with me as soon as possible.'

'Do you think it will happen? Do you think we'll all be together?' Janey asked, and Nina thought for a moment, not as a frantic sister but as the social worker she was. She was their sister who *finally* had a three-bedroomed flat, an older sister who, though it would be incredibly strained financially, actually could support them, there were no protective issues, the children wanted to be there and finally, after all these years,

Nina was able to look her sister in the eye and give her real hope.

'I do,' Nina said. 'I actually do.' And she gave Janey a cuddle, knew that nothing was guaranteed, but for the first time Nina allowed herself to get excited. She didn't say it, didn't want to make a promise that she might not get to keep, but she thought it. *Janey, I swear you and Blake are coming home to me.*

Jack was quiet on the drive home and quiet again when she told him he could just drop her off there.

'I want to talk to you, Nina.'

He followed her in.

'Thanks again for tonight—'

'Things will get sorted now,' Jack said. 'I'm sorry Janey had to go through all that...' He saw her struggle to blink back the tears, moved in to hold her, but she shrugged him off.

'I'm really not up for talking, Jack.'

'Fair enough.' His mouth grazed hers, his eyes open and watching hers close, not in bliss but in reluctant acceptance. He felt her tongue in his mouth and her hands move down to his crotch, he heard her fake moan to arouse when she realised that he wasn't hard, and if Jack had been angry before, he was furious now.

'Don't...' She heard the anger in his voice as he removed her hand. 'Don't you ever just go through the motions with me.'

He saw the burn on her cheeks as his fury built inside and he struggled to contain it.

'Did I earn it tonight?' Jack asked, and he struggled not to shout. 'Are you just trying to get it over and done with?'

'Leave if you don't like it.'

And he saw her gutter mouth come out for him, because that was where she'd almost been, saw the scared angry kid she had once been. 'When you say you haven't had a relationship for a long time…' She pushed past him, but he caught her. 'When was the last time you had sex, Nina?'

'Friday night, from memory.' She opened the door. 'Just leave.'

'Before then,' Jack said. 'Before us.'

Nina stood holding the door open, but Jack would not move.

'A while.' Nina shrugged.

'Oh, I think it was a while,' Jack said. 'I'd say about six years. Is that what the pro bono centre did for you? They got you off the streets…'

'I wasn't a hooker, Jack,' she snarled, 'if that's what you're thinking.' He saw all the anger shooting from her eyes and it was merited. 'But there can be a lot of favours to pay for sleeping on a friend's couch…' And then she started to cry.

'And was I the first since that time?' She just stood there.

'What was I supposed to say?' Nina shouted. 'That you're the first person I've even considered fancying, that for two years I've had a thing for you…?' She just looked at him. 'You'd have run a mile.'

Jack didn't know how to deal with this. He just stood there confused, because it *had* been so much more than sex that night.

'Can you please leave?' she said when he walked over to her. 'I mean it,' she said, still holding the door. 'Jack, can you leave?'

And, given what she'd just told him, Jack had no choice but to respect her wishes, no choice really but to do as she asked and leave.

Jack was angry.

More than angry and there wasn't even an actual person he could pin it on. He had been angry enough with what had happened to Janey, but that it had happened to Nina, that there hadn't been an older sister looking out for her, that she had been left to her own devices had Jack's mind working overtime.

There was no one he could speak to about it either.

Jack tried to imagine the reaction of his parents if he tried to talk about what had happened with Nina.

The sneers, the turning up of their noses.

But he knew that the last thing Nina needed was to see that. He had to deal with this himself, had to work out how best to handle it.

Nina's cheeks fired the next morning when she saw him in the corridor and she just brushed past him. They fired up again a few hours later when her intercom buzzed and Jack was at her door.

And she blushed even more when he sat in the chair where she'd, er, once approached him. And then he did the impossible, just as he had the first time he'd come to her office. Jack made her laugh.

'Is the chair okay or do you want me on the mat again?'

'Very funny, Jack.' She laughed, but she was still cringing about what she had told him last night.

'Nina, don't ignore me in the corridor again. I told you, I don't do awkward,' Jack said, simply addressing the situation between them.

'Thank you.'

And then Jack got to another reason he was there.

'I heard their might be some news.'

There was. The news was still fluttering in her chest, still new and shiny and hard to take in, and she hadn't actually said the words out loud yet.

'I've got custody…' She was shaking just saying it. All those years of study and work and scrimping and saving, just to get to this point, and finally, sooner than expected, she could say it. 'It's temporary custody for now, but they've been to look at the flat, and apparently Blake isn't happy where he is.' She hated so much what they had all been through. 'They're not horrible people or anything, they're just older and can't deal with him…'

'You've got them now.' Jack came and leant on the desk beside her chair. 'They're good kids.'

'They are!' Nina was adamant on that. 'I know Janey can be a handful, but I'm really going to work on her. I'm going to show the department just how much better she is with me.'

And he knew he had to step back here, that it wasn't his place to tell her how to raise them. After all, what would he know? Professionally, yes, he had his opinion, but on family…? He thought of his own family, the complete dysfunction behind the smiling façade, but more than that he needed to do some serious thinking.

Serious thinking.

'Say hi to them for me.' He gave a thin smile. 'Tell them I'll come by and see them some time soon.'

'I think we need some time together...' She saw him frown, saw the slight startlement in his eyes and realised he'd misunderstood what she had said, that he must have thought she was working out a way to schedule some alone time for them, so she made things a little clearer. 'Not us.' God, it hurt to lose him. 'Me and the kids. We need some time to settle in with each other and...' She gave him a smile when she felt like weeping. 'Really, Jack, it might just confuse things if you keep coming round.'

'Yeah, well, I told Blake that I'd get him a Rangers top,' Jack said.

'You can give that to me at work.'

'And I also said to Janey that I'd check in and see that she was okay, wherever she was...so, tough, I'm coming round.'

He walked back through the hospital and popped into ICU before heading for home, and for Jack things couldn't be more confusing.

He was being dumped and surely he should be sighing with relief, cracking open the champagne and celebrating, because Jack Carter with a twenty-five-year-old, anti-fashion girlfriend, who came with two messed-up kids in tow was so not part of the plan.

And he was still confused when he got home and looked around his tastefully furnished apartment, because all it looked was sterile. He looked into the mirror as he shaved the next morning, saw the fading bruise and decided that if he saw Vince again he'd happily repeat the experience.

He wanted something more from this relationship, wanted something he had never known, and, no, he didn't understand it.

CHAPTER TWELVE

NINA DIDN'T SAY his name. Instead, she pursed her lips when on Friday night Jack came to her door just as she was about to start dinner.

'I rang your office.' Jack smiled. 'They said you left at five.'

'I did.' Nina tried to move out to the hall so that Blake and Janey wouldn't realise that he was there. 'I've got a lot to do, Jack—there's a lot to unpack.' She still hadn't set up the chests of drawers in Janey's room, but she wasn't going to tell him that.

'I thought I might help. Maybe I could go out and get dinner.' He sniffed the air. 'Is that chicken? I thought you didn't eat meat.'

He spoke too loudly so she did move out into the hall as there was no way she wanted Blake to hear him. 'Just because I'm vegetarian it doesn't mean that they have to be.'

'Jack!' Like a Jack-seeking missile, Blake came out to the hall. 'Did you get my top?'

'Blake.' Nina was stern. 'Don't be rude.'

'It's fine,' Jack said. 'No, I haven't got your top yet. I'm working on it.'

He'd probably get one signed by the whole hockey team. Nina could just picture it.

'Are you going to ask me in?' Jack said. 'Or is it chicken for two?'

It was a chicken for three and Nina just had the vegetables. It worried her how much Blake adored him. Janey even asked him for some help with her homework a bit later and Nina heard him ask if she knew what she wanted to do in the future.

'No idea,' Janey admitted. 'Anyway, I think I might have left it too late to get good grades.'

'You're fifteen,' Jack said. 'It's not too late to turn things around. You just need to focus.'

After dinner Nina thanked him for coming over and though she did it nicely it was clear she was asking him to leave.

'I'll be off, then. Oh, and, Nina...' he gave her a smile '...you do remember that you agreed to go to the dinner dance tomorrow for the burns unit...?'

'I didn't agree,' Nina said.

'Well, it's a bit too late to back out now—I've put your name down, bought the tickets...' Annoyingly he smiled. 'It's for a very good cause.'

'I can babysit,' Janey chimed in, before Nina could use that as an excuse, but she shook her head.

'I'm not going out your first Saturday night here and leaving you to babysit.'

'Why not?' Jack asked, and she wished he would just butt out. She could hardly stand here and say that she didn't know if she trusted Janey, but she had no choice but to agree, making it clear that she'd rather he went home now.

'I'll pick you up at seven,' Jack said, and then said goodbye to Blake and Janey.

'You were mean,' Blake said accusingly.

'I wasn't mean,' Nina said, but it was said rather forcibly to override her disquiet, because Jack had seemed to genuinely want to be there and yet again it had been a good evening.

'That's how I used to feel,' Blake said when she went in later to kiss him goodnight.

'When?'

'At Dianne's. I always felt that she just wanted to get back to her family.'

'It's not like that with Jack.' Nina did her best to explain what she didn't herself understand. 'Jack's a very good friend.'

'He's more than your friend.'

'Yes,' Nina said carefully.

'So why were you mean to him?'

'I wasn't mean. The thing is, Jack comes from a very well-to-do family, he's a very…' She stopped because it was impossible to explain.

'You said things like that don't matter.'

'They don't.' Nina blew out a breath. How could she tell Blake that Jack couldn't possibly be ready for this ready-made family? That really, as fun as the time had been that they'd had together, it would be marked in days, weeks at best.

There was not just one but three hearts that could be very easily broken here if she wasn't careful.

'Let's just worry about us for now.' She gave him a kiss goodnight.

'What are you wearing for the dinner?' Janey asked when Nina came out from saying goodnight to Blake.

'I'm not sure yet.'

'Are you going to buy something?'

Nina shook her head. She was already worrying enough about dropping her hours, without buying a new dress, and anyway nothing she could afford could even begin to match the lavish women that would be there.

No, things like that shouldn't matter, but it was going to be an embarrassing way to prove a point.

'There's a nice retro store I know. They have some top-end stuff,' Janey suggested. 'We could go shopping tomorrow.'

And it was the most *normal* suggestion Janey had made, just two sisters going shopping, and of course Blake would come along too but, yes, the thought of having some quality time with Janey and possibly finding a dress that wasn't going to make her stand out like a sore thumb worked on so many levels that less than twelve hours later Nina found herself being bullied to try on dresses that were absolutely not her style.

'It's nice,' Nina said, because it was the best of the bunch, 'but...' She turned around in the mirror and wasn't quite so sure. It was a chocolate-brown dress that looked great from the front but from the back showed rather too much of her spine. She thought of the glossed and buffed women who would be attending, women who would have spent ages in preparation, and suddenly Nina felt more than a little nervous. She had no interest in competing with them, but at the same time she didn't want to embarrass Jack.

'You've got shoes that will go with it,' Janey reminded her. 'And I'm also starving.'

'So am I,' Blake said, thoroughly bored by the whole shopping expedition. 'When can we go home?'

'Okay, okay,' Nina said, but pleased with her purchase she was actually glad Janey had suggested that they come here, and once home and eating lunch she told her so.

'I enjoyed it,' Janey admitted, and then looked at the clock. 'You'd better start getting ready.'

'He's not picking me up till six.' It had been seven p.m. that Jack was to pick her up but he'd texted that morning with a last-minute change of plans. They were going to stop by and have drinks at his parents' house and then go to the dinner from there. The thought of meeting his parents was more daunting than what would follow.

'Which gives you four hours,' Janey pointed out. 'You've no idea, have you?' Janey just stared at her older sister. 'Some of these women will have spent days preparing for this.'

'Okay, okay.'

'And you're going to his posh parents' house—you'll have to look nice for that too.' Janey actually laughed. 'I can't believe he's taking you to meet his family.'

'It's nothing like that.' Oh, she knew better than to read anything into it. The Carters were sociable people and no doubt wanted to briefly meet her before they shared an evening at the same table but, still, it was for that reason that she allowed Janey to paint her finger- and toenails *and* let her do her hair.

'I don't want it straightened,' Nina said as Janey plugged her equipment in.

'I'm not going to straighten it.' Janey rolled her eyes at her very out-of-date older sister. 'I'm going to give you curls.'

Which she did.

Over and over she pulled the straighteners and it was nice to sit in the bedroom as Janey got to work and just chat, to find out that this was the sort of thing Janey liked to get up to with her friends, just spend the evening doing hair and nails and things; that beneath that scowling expression and black eyeliner was actually a very young, very nice young girl. It made her heart thump in her chest to think of what might have happened if Jack hadn't handled things so well.

'You should have a few friends over one night,' Nina suggested as Janey got to work on her make-up.

'So you can interrogate them?'

'No. So you can have some fun with them here.'

'Tonight?'

'No.' Nina knew Janey was teasing, because they'd had some very long conversations. 'Tonight you're in charge of Blake and I'm trusting you to get this right.'

'You mean Jack's trusting me.'

'Okay,' Nina admitted. 'Maybe he did push for it, but I think he's right—you're nearly sixteen you should be able to look after your brother. I'll be home before midnight. Go easy with the make-up,' Nina said, pulling away.

'I have,' Janey said. 'You're done! But you need to see it with your dress and shoes on and everything.'

Nina was somewhat nervous going over to the mirror. While she was all for encouraging Janey, she didn't want to go out tonight looking like a complete clown, but when she stood in the hall and stared into the long mirror she didn't comment for a while.

'You like it, don't you?'

Nina did like it, perhaps because she barely recognised herself.

Her hair, which she usually pinned up loosely or pulled back now fell in loose ringlets and her make-up was amazing. It had felt as if Janey was putting far too much on, but actually it was all very subtle. Her skin looked creamy and her eye shadow was brown, which brought out her deep blue eyes, and her lips were a pinkish neutral. The only place Janey had been heavy with was the eyelashes. From long, fair and invisible, they were now soft and black and really long, and however she looked in the mirror she knew that there was no way she could have put this all together herself.

'You're really good at this.'

'I know.'

'I mean,' Nina said slowly, '*really* good at this.'

'Are you nervous?' Janey asked.

'A bit,' Nina admitted.

'Maybe Jack is,' Janey said, but Nina shook her head.

'These things are no big deal to Jack. He won't be giving it a second thought.'

She could not have been more wrong.

As his driver brought him closer to Nina's, Jack was having serious second thoughts.

He must have been mad to suggest that she come to his parents' for drinks—a table at dinner would have been fine, but to bring her into his home? He'd been thinking of himself, wanting to show Nina first hand what was so hard to explain, except he hadn't properly considered the effect it might have on Nina...until now.

He could just imagine his mother's disapproving eye as she saw Nina in an off-the-peg number. He wouldn't put it past her to even question out loud if her was dress was suitable for tonight.

As the car stopped outside Nina's apartment Jack climbed out and even as he took the lift he wondered if he should suggest they stay at her apartment for a while and just meet his parents at the venue.

'Hey, Jack...' Blake let him in. 'She's been getting ready for ages.'

'You're not supposed to tell me that.' Jack winked. 'Trust me on that one. Here...' He handed him a bag and smiled at Blake's expression and shout of delight as he took out the top. He hadn't had it signed by the entire team but there was Blake's favourite player's signature and a signed photo, and the little guy was so excited he dashed off to show his sisters, leaving Jack standing in the hallway. And after a moment he let himself in.

'I hope you said thank you.'

Jack said nothing. He wasn't trying to get Blake into trouble, but for a moment there he actually forgot he had a voice, because she looked nothing like he could have expected—she looked incredible. Still Nina, still different, but she would turn heads for different reasons tonight.

'You look amazing.'

'Thanks to Janey,' Nina said.

'Thank you, Janey.' Jack smiled.

'So am I going to get paid for being personal shopper, make-up artist and babysitter?' Janey asked as Nina filled her bag.

'No,' Nina said. 'That's what....' She gave in then. Janey had saved her a fortune tonight and in years to come she had her own personal stylist under her roof. What wasn't to love? So she gave her some money and didn't notice that Jack gave her some too, but with a warning that he expected her on her most responsible behaviour tonight.

'I will be,' Janey insisted. 'I want Nina to have a good time.'

So did Jack.

For the hundredth time he wondered what the hell he was doing. He actually felt a bit sick as the car approached his family home, the same nausea he had always felt at the beginning of the school holidays, knowing he would have to spend the summer here, or Christmas...

Jack had far preferred his time at boarding school.

'I'm nervous...' Nina said.

'I know.' Jack helped her out of the car. 'They're pretty daunting.'

It wasn't the answer Nina had been expecting. She'd hoped he'd reassure her that it was no big deal, that he brought friends home all the time, that they'd met so many of his girlfriends that they'd struggle to remember her name for the night, but he said nothing, just took her arm and led her to a front door she'd seen pictured on the covers of lifestyle magazines and Sunday papers and that soon would admit her.

'They're used to this, though.' She was speaking more for her own benefit than his, trying to reassure herself when he didn't. 'You'd have brought a lot of women here.'

'I've never brought anyone back here.' She turned and frowned just as she heard someone approach from the other side of the door. 'I've never brought a friend home, even when I was at school, and certainly I've never brought a date back here.'

'Never?'

'Never,' Jack said. 'And I'm really sorry to put you through this.'

She had no idea what he was talking about.

The door was opened by a servant, who took their coats, and Jack led her through a house that was huge. Then she stepped into the gorgeous lounge that she had seen in the pages of a magazine.

'Jack…' His mother turned as he walked in. She was sipping a glass of champagne and chatting on the phone, but she muted it for a moment and naturally Nina recognised her and gave her a smile.

'Mother, this is Nina Wilson.'

She gave a brief nod in her conversation and it was Jack who introduced her. 'Nina, this is Anna,' he said as she resumed talking on the telephone, bitching about the guests that were going tonight. Nina sat there, cheeks scalding, stunned as everything she thought she knew about the Carters was wiped out of existence.

The father walked in and Jack Carter Senior sort of gave a brief nod in their direction and snapped for a maid to hurry up with his drink.

'What time are we leaving?' were his first words to Jack.

'We're to be there for seven-thirty, so soon,' Jack said, as Nina realised exactly why Jack had been in no hurry to leave her place. They were the coldest, most distant people Nina had ever met. Everything she had read or seen had been an complete act. This was so not the all American family they portrayed.

They were dismissive way past the point of rudeness.

His mother came off the phone but made no attempt to speak with either Jack or Nina, just checked a few details with her husband. They might just as well have not been there, though Jack did make an effort.

He introduced Nina to his father.

Jack Senior just gave a vague nod in her direction.

'Nina does a lot of work at the pro bono centre in Harlem.'

Anna wrinkled up her nose, but Jack pushed on. 'Did you know Louis Cavel donates some time there?'

'I've heard.' Jack Senior nodded. 'I did consider it, of course it would look good, but really...' He shook his head and looked at Nina. 'I suppose you're always looking for donations.'

'We prefer people's time,' Nina responded, but the thought of spending time with this man, knowing it was simply a matter of looking good, and she was more than happy to bend the rules for him. 'Of course donations are always welcome.'

'Louis puts a lot of hours in,' Jack persisted. 'He does scar reductions, resets noses, you really should see the work he does with victims of domestic violence. There's an amazing body of people there...'

'There's a far simpler solution,' Anna said. 'If these women just left their husbands in the first place, they could save us a whole lot of trouble.' Anna laughed at her own joke and her husband laughed too, and Nina realised why Jack had apologised in advance for them—it was truly painful to be there.

The maid came and announced that the car was ready for them and as they stood Anna asked a question. 'What's the dinner in aid of tonight?' she asked.

'The burns unit at Angel's,' Jack said, and his mother gave a little shudder.

'God, I hope they don't do a presentation.'

They were disgusting.

There was no other word for them and Nina was so glad they were travelling in separate cars and had some time alone with Jack before they arrived at the dinner. Nina, who would never usually speak in front of the driver, actually didn't care tonight. He presumably knew the real Carters behind the sparkling façade.

'Are they always like that?'

Jack didn't look at her. He was acutely embarrassed. Nina was the first person he had brought home and his parents had actually been quite civil.

'Believe me, that was nothing.'

'Is that why you don't bring anyone home?' Nina asked. 'Because you're embarrassed that it might get out...?'

'I couldn't care less,' Jack said. 'There's a strange unspoken rule that what happens at home stays at home but, really, that's not why I've kept people away. I've dated more than a few women who would have happily joined in that conversation.'

'Were they always like that?'

'Always.' Jack nodded. 'Sorry to ruin your night.'

'Thanks a lot.' Nina smiled back.

As they walked into the function she watched his parents turn on the charm and work the room in glittering style, and yet she knew how twenty minutes in their company had made her feel.

Imagine growing up with that?

The place was beautifully decorated, the table gleaming with silverware and gorgeous little chocolate mice, which, Nina found out when she took a bite, were filled with the most amazing mousse. Everything was beautiful or rather, Nina now realised, everything appeared to be.

They sat and ate and chatted and laughed and Nina played her part. They were at a table for twelve and Anna was beguiling them all, and she turned her beams on Nina.

'Stunning dress...'

'Thank you.'

'I can't quite place it.'

'Neither could the sales assistant,' Nina answered. 'The label had been ripped out.' And she made it clear she had bought it at the retro store. Jack watched his mother's face flush beneath her make-up, her eyes shooting angrily to Jack, but he just leant back in his chair, his arm draped loosely over the back of Nina's chair as she carried on with her dinner. 'I offered to get her a dress, but the thing is with Nina, she'd never spend that sort of money on fashion...'

'Very commendable…' Anna gave a vinegar smile.

And while Nina didn't need his mother's approval, his mother felt the need to assure Nina that she'd never have it, or at least to score a few points, because she needled away at Nina when Jack got up to make a speech.

'Yet, for all your altruism, you're happy to sit in your second-hand dress and eat the finest food and drink the best champagne…'

'Very happy to.' Nina met her cool glare. 'It was nice of Jack to invite me and I'm very touched that he did. I work with a lot of families on the burns unit, and this fundraiser will help a lot.'

And she turned from what was unimportant to someone who was, and listened as Jack made his speech. It wasn't a particularly emotional speech. It wasn't designed to pull at the heartstrings but it was to the point and funny at times, and from the reaction of the room just what had been needed to make it a successful evening.

Jack watched the conversation taking place at his table, saw his mother attempting to smile for the room as Nina crushed her with a few words. He had been so right to bring her. Jack knew then that all the doubts of the past few days faded as he had met the one woman who could stand up to his family, because Nina truly did not care what they thought of her. She was the one woman he had met who really was not turned on by money, which meant, Jack realised as they danced a little later, she was turned on only by him.

'Sorry about that,' he said, and she pulled back her face and looked up at him.

'You have *nothing* to apologise for,' she said. 'I might, though. I think I was a bit rude…'

'She has a very thick skin,' Jack assured her. 'Can you do me a favour?'

'Of course.'

'Can you feign a headache?'

'No feigning required.'

They weren't actually leaving that early. People were already starting to drift off. His mother was grimly wringing the last out of the champagne bottle and rather than anger Jack felt an immense sadness as he wished his parents goodnight.

They simply had no idea what was real, and he was only just finding out.

They didn't take a car but walked instead, through the city they both loved but had experienced through very different eyes.

'I'm going to volunteer at the centre,' Jack said. 'Well, I'm going to apply to.'

'Can you afford the time?'

'Not at the moment,' he admitted, 'but I can cut back on some other things.' They sat in Central Park and looked at the couples going past on the last of the night carriage rides and then up to Angel's and all that was going on unseen behind the windows. 'I don't think I'm right as Head of Paeds,' Jack admitted. 'The board is happy because I'm bringing in a lot of funds but, really, my role should be more hands on…'

'You can make it that way.'

'I'm going to,' Jack said. 'I'm going to pull back on

the fundraising stuff and put in some hours at the pro bono centre, but I don't think I'm practising medicine the way I want to. I know I'm good at what I do, but…' he let out a breath '…I want to do more.'

'You will, then,' Nina said. She had, for so long, thought him cold and arrogant and, yes, in recent times she had seen a different side to him, but tonight she really was starting to understand why Jack was the way he was. 'What was it like, growing up with them?'

'Messed up,' Jack said. 'But at the time you think it's normal. I was told off for crying, for any display of emotion really. I think I finally worked out how far from normal it was when I was eight and stayed with that family for a week. I saw how different things should be.'

'Yet you didn't go and stay with them at Christmas?'

'Because it's easier not to know how bad things really are sometimes,' Jack explained. 'I understand how angry Janey was last week—how an amazing weekend away just made it harder to go back—that was how I felt after my holiday.'

'So much for the perfect family,' Nina said. 'Maybe there is no such thing.'

They hailed a cab and as they approached her apartment Jack just sat there as Nina went to climb out.

'Aren't you coming in?'

'Am I invited?' Jack asked, and Nina took a breath.

'For coffee.'

'Then yes.'

Blake was asleep and Janey was watching a movie, but after a brief chat she went off yawning to bed.

'Here.' Nina handed him his coffee and she felt incredibly awkward, embarrassed to be alone with him, with the man who knew so much about her past.

But was somehow still there.

Jack looked around the shabby apartment that had been so fought for and cherished by three people, and he knew why—it was home.

'Thanks for these past couple of weeks, Jack.' Nina made herself say it. 'I really do mean that.'

'You're welcome,' Jack said, and took a mouthful of coffee before speaking. 'Thank you too.'

'For what?' Nina grinned.

'Oh, a few things spring to mind—changing my career path for one.'

'Sorry about that.'

He drained his coffee. 'I'm going to go.'

He really ought to do exactly that, the sensible part of him knew that as he stood, or rather the sensible part of the Jack he had been a couple of weeks ago, who had looked out at the ward and chastised himself for even considering a fling with Nina Wilson, knew that he should just get out now. Except he'd done more thinking these past weeks than he had in a long time, and more thinking that he'd ever thought he would about a woman in the days since she'd asked him to leave.

''Night, Nina.'

He moved in to give her a kiss, just a friendly kiss that started on her cheek and then moved to her mouth, and she felt the graze of his lips, felt her own tremble to his mouth, but then he removed it.

''Night.' He smiled and his arms let her go.

Except she wanted some more of his mouth.

'Jack…' she called as he headed to the door. 'You said things would never be awkward between us.'

'They won't be,' he assured her.

'You don't have to go,' Nina said. 'I mean, if you want…'

'Tell me what you want, Nina.'

Her cheeks burnt as she said it, as she told him exactly what she would like to happen. 'I'd like you to stay.'

'Or we could just have a kiss and see where that leads?'

And her cheeks burnt some more. She felt the wrap of his arms around her and then his lovely mouth and she kissed him in a way she never had. His tongue slid around hers and his mouth tasted divine, so she kept right on kissing until it wasn't enough, till she wanted him to kiss her harder, but still he just kissed her slowly and when her hands left his hair and tried to work down his body, Jack halted them, held them down by her sides and just kept kissing her till she though she might die from the pleasure. She gave in then, till the pleasure was too much and not enough at the same time, and Nina pressed her body into him, except Jack pushed her hips back and then stopped.

'What do you want, Nina?'

'I want you to stay.'

'In that case,' Jack said, 'I'd love to.'

And he entered the hallowed turf of her bedroom and kissed her again, just as blissfully as he had out in the hall, except she wanted more.

'Jack…' His hands were back holding hers down. 'Please.'

'What do you want, Nina?'

'For you to undress me.'

'I'd love to.'

And he was way too slow, just so painfully slow because she wanted to be on the bed with him, but instead he was slowly unzipping her dress and then taking off her underwear, very, very slowly, with no kisses in between. His touch was tender, just not enough, and when he knelt down and carefully took off her shoes, she could have wept at the slight graze of his hair on her thighs when she wanted his mouth.

'Please, Jack…' She went to the buttons of his shirt, but his hands stopped her. 'Please.'

So he undressed himself while still kissing her and frantically she helped him, closing her eyes to the bliss of their naked skin pressed together and she simply could not stay standing and she knew what he was doing and just gave in to it now.

'I want you to take me to bed.'

'I'd love to.'

And Jack was old enough to dress himself, and she watched and held onto his shoulders as he protected them then kissed her, moving her onto the bed. She wanted to hold him, to touch him, yet still he restrained her. Then he began to move his hands over her body, until she was crying and dizzy, and then his hands were still and hers led him to where she wanted them to be, because tonight it was all about her.

'What do you want, Nina?

'You to…' His hand went over her mouth and he spoke into her ear and reminded her she was a lady. He felt her mouth stretch on his palm into a smile and then he felt the heat of her skin as it flared into a dark blush.

'What do you want?' he checked.

'For you to make love to me.'

And so he did, and Nina didn't care about tomorrow as he moved inside her, as he took her completely, because whatever happened from this point he had given her tonight—a night when she didn't hold back, when she moaned and writhed beneath him. And Jack didn't hold back either. Maybe it would be awkward at work in the future because, when they came, he was telling her he loved her and she was telling him the same. Afterwards they lay there, Nina burning from the pleasure and just a bit embarrassed because, yes, she loved him, she just hadn't really wanted him to know how much.

'What do you want, Nina?'

She frowned and turned her head to him, had thought that delicious game was over.

'Tell me,' he insisted.

She looked at the playboy on her pillow and would love him for ever, but she knew there were limits, knew that the truth couldn't fully come out here. 'What I can't have.'

'How do you know that?'

'I know that.' She smiled, and watched as he turned onto his elbow and then gave her a little telling-off.

'You need to start saying what you want,' Jack said. 'You need to be able to say what you want.'

'I know that.'

'So say it.'

'I'd like to see more of you.'

'How much more?'

'I don't know.'

'I think you do.'

'And I think it's impossible...' She forced another smile. 'I've effectively got two kids...'

'Forget them.'

'I can't,' Nina sobbed, because she couldn't and never would, even if it meant that she and Jack couldn't have a future together.

'Forget about your brother and sister and my reaction, and just tell me what it is that you want.' Jack was insistent.

And at the risk of him running from the bed and grabbing his suit, at the absolute risk of him running off and life being terribly awkward in the morning, she told him.

'I want you to be a part of my family.' She said it and Jack listened and he didn't run. He'd done that in the past few days when he had carefully thought about all he might be about to take on, and as he looked down Jack knew he had come to the right decision and her honesty only proved it now.

'I'd love to be.'

'Don't say that...' She didn't want a heat of-the-moment thing, she told him.

'It isn't,' Jack assured her. 'I've thought about it, I've done nothing but think about it, and, yes, it's a bit overwhelming, but...' He had never been so honest either. He told her about Monica the other night, how empty he had felt, how empty he had been till she'd come into his life.

'Your mother's going to hate me!' Nina grinned, starting to believe this might be true.

'I know.' Jack grinned. 'I just can't wait to tell her!'

And then he told her that he was going to go and buy a ring, but figured she'd want to choose… 'I can't really win,' Jack moaned. 'If I spend too much you'll get upset, but I'm not donating for trees somewhere or buying goats instead, like I know you'll suggest. I want to take you out and spoil you.'

'How can I say no to that?'

'You can't.'

She couldn't.

So, instead, Nina said yes.

EPILOGUE

JACK LOVED FRIDAYS.

He always had and he always would, but he was especially looking forward to this one.

Blake and Janey were off at summer camp and tonight he and Nina were flying to Hawaii for a delayed honeymoon. He walked up the garden path of their large Brooklyn home after a very full week working at the pro bono centre.

Nina had been right.

His rather more analytical mind had been exactly what the centre had needed and Jack was part of the team that allocated funds as well as running two night clinics a week, and he loved it.

Jack didn't miss Angel's. He was often there, consulting on a patient he'd had admitted or stopping by to take Nina for lunch.

'How was work?' Jack asked as Nina woke up from a doze, stretched on the sofa and yawned.

'Exhausting,' she admitted. 'I think I got everything done before we go away, but the trouble with working part time is that you end up doing a full week's work in half the time. Though it was a good day. I saw Tommy and Mike...'

'And?'

'Tommy's finished his chemotherapy and the doctors are really pleased with the results.'

'Is he having surgery?'

'I'm not sure,' Nina said. 'I think there's a big case meeting next week, but for now, at least, things are going better than expected.'

Everything was going better than expected.

Nina had been a Carter for a few months now, but as of this week so too were Janey and Blake. A few days after they'd announced they were getting married, Janey had flared up at something, and shouted that Jack had no say, that he was only her sister's boyfriend, or her brother-in-law.

'We'll see about that!' Jack had snapped back, and so earlier in the week they'd all stood in front of a judge who had smiled as broadly as all of them for the photo to capture the moment Jack officially became a father.

And now Nina had to somehow tell him that he was about to become a father again.

She didn't know how she felt about it, had wanted to wait a while, but that option was closed to them now.

'So,' Jack said, 'are we packed?'

'I am.' Nina smiled.

She followed him into their bedroom and he laughed when he opened the case because it contained two bikinis, a sarong and not much else. Jack threw in a couple of things too.

They would have their own very private pool and had no intention to leave its side.

'It's going to be nice to have some time on our own,' Nina said, but Jack didn't really comment. He loved the busy household they had made, loved doing sport with Blake and just having a childhood thirty years late. He knew she was fishing, knew Nina was waiting for him to admit it was too much at times.

He never did.

Still, there were some advantages to having the house to themselves, because he had her try on her new bikini and then had the pleasure of taking it off, and all without having to think and close the door, and afterwards, as his hands traced her body, he noticed the tiny changes, the slight fullness to her breasts, and he wondered when she was going to tell him.

'We'd better get ready.' He caught her as she went to get off the bed, and pulled her back to him.

'When are you going to tell me?'

He watched the colour spread first on her cheeks and then down to her chest, watched her rapid, confused blink. 'What?'

'That I'm going to be a father of three?' Jack smiled. 'How long have you been holding out on me?'

'Jack!' she wailed in frustration. This wasn't how it was supposed to be. 'I was going to tell you on holiday...' She shook her head in exasperation. 'I only found out this afternoon.'

'I've known for a week.' Jack grinned. 'I thought you just weren't telling me. I knew at the courtroom....

'How?'

'I can't tell you.'

'You can.'

'I really can't.' Jack grinned. 'Because you'll accuse me of being a chauvinist.'

'You are a chauvinist!' Nina reminded him. 'But

I'm working on it.' She didn't understand. 'How did you know before I did?'

'You forget sometimes that you're married to a brilliant diagnostician,' Jack said. 'Okay, I'll tell you. Remember our case was pushed back, remember how that woman in the coffee shop pushed in line…?'

'Yes.' She was sulking before he said it.

'And it was a tense day and I knew that your period was due, but you were lovely…'

'Don't!' Nina dug him the ribs with her elbows. 'Don't you dare…'

'I'm not,' Jack said. 'I'm just saying…'

And he was arrogant and rude and chauvinistic at times, but he was also the best thing to have happened in her life and she wouldn't change a single piece of him.

'Are you okay with it?'

'Delighted,' Jack said. 'Who'd have thought that night when we rowed that in a few months I'd be married, a father of two, with one on the way, and we haven't even been on our honeymoon yet?'

'Me,' Nina broke in, and for the first time she told him the truth, a truth she'd kept hidden from herself.

That it hadn't been just a crush that she'd had, and she hadn't just fancied him either, that the whole problem she'd had was…

'I loved you from the start.'

* * * * *

Mills & Boon® Hardback
March 2013

ROMANCE

Playing the Dutiful Wife	Carol Marinelli
The Fallen Greek Bride	Jane Porter
A Scandal, a Secret, a Baby	Sharon Kendrick
The Notorious Gabriel Diaz	Cathy Williams
A Reputation For Revenge	Jennie Lucas
Captive in the Spotlight	Annie West
Taming the Last Acosta	Susan Stephens
Island of Secrets	Robyn Donald
The Taming of a Wild Child	Kimberly Lang
First Time For Everything	Aimee Carson
Guardian to the Heiress	Margaret Way
Little Cowgirl on His Doorstep	Donna Alward
Mission: Soldier to Daddy	Soraya Lane
Winning Back His Wife	Melissa McClone
The Guy To Be Seen With	Fiona Harper
Why Resist a Rebel?	Leah Ashton
Sydney Harbour Hospital: Evie's Bombshell	Amy Andrews
The Prince Who Charmed Her	Fiona McArthur

MEDICAL

NYC Angels: Redeeming The Playboy	Carol Marinelli
NYC Angels: Heiress's Baby Scandal	Janice Lynn
St Piran's: The Wedding!	Alison Roberts
His Hidden American Beauty	Connie Cox

Mills & Boon® Large Print

March 2013

ROMANCE

A Night of No Return	Sarah Morgan
A Tempestuous Temptation	Cathy Williams
Back in the Headlines	Sharon Kendrick
A Taste of the Untamed	Susan Stephens
The Count's Christmas Baby	Rebecca Winters
His Larkville Cinderella	Melissa McClone
The Nanny Who Saved Christmas	Michelle Douglas
Snowed in at the Ranch	Cara Colter
Exquisite Revenge	Abby Green
Beneath the Veil of Paradise	Kate Hewitt
Surrendering All But Her Heart	Melanie Milburne

HISTORICAL

How to Sin Successfully	Bronwyn Scott
Hattie Wilkinson Meets Her Match	Michelle Styles
The Captain's Kidnapped Beauty	Mary Nichols
The Admiral's Penniless Bride	Carla Kelly
Return of the Border Warrior	Blythe Gifford

MEDICAL

Her Motherhood Wish	Anne Fraser
A Bond Between Strangers	Scarlet Wilson
Once a Playboy...	Kate Hardy
Challenging the Nurse's Rules	Janice Lynn
The Sheikh and the Surrogate Mum	Meredith Webber
Tamed by her Brooding Boss	Joanna Neil

Mills & Boon® Hardback

April 2013

ROMANCE

Master of her Virtue	Miranda Lee
The Cost of her Innocence	Jacqueline Baird
A Taste of the Forbidden	Carole Mortimer
Count Valieri's Prisoner	Sara Craven
The Merciless Travis Wilde	Sandra Marton
A Game with One Winner	Lynn Raye Harris
Heir to a Desert Legacy	Maisey Yates
The Sinful Art of Revenge	Maya Blake
Marriage in Name Only?	Anne Oliver
Waking Up Married	Mira Lyn Kelly
Sparks Fly with the Billionaire	Marion Lennox
A Daddy for Her Sons	Raye Morgan
Along Came Twins...	Rebecca Winters
An Accidental Family	Ami Weaver
A Date with a Bollywood Star	Riya Lakhani
The Proposal Plan	Charlotte Phillips
Their Most Forbidden Fling	Melanie Milburne
The Last Doctor She Should Ever Date	Louisa George

MEDICAL

NYC Angels: Unmasking Dr Serious	Laura Iding
NYC Angels: The Wallflower's Secret	Susan Carlisle
Cinderella of Harley Street	Anne Fraser
You, Me and a Family	Sue MacKay

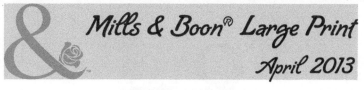

Mills & Boon® Large Print

April 2013

ROMANCE

HISTORICAL

MEDICAL